The Wasatch Savage

The Wasatch Savage

by Lee Nelson

Liberty Press

ISBN # 0-936860-20-0

Printed in the United States of America
First Printing January, 1984

"Do I dare disturb the universe?"

--T. S. Eliot

The Wasatch Savage

Chapter 1

Bill Thunder sat quietly on the top rail of the circular corral just south of the bunkhouse on the Medicine Horse Ranch near Bear River, Utah. The late afternoon sun pressed warmly against the back of his red and black wool shirt.

Bill looked toward the chute across the corral. A wild-eyed Indian youth with unruly wind-tossed hair and a torn blue denim jacket was lowering himself onto the back of a restless yearling calf that he was determined to ride before the day was through. Two other boys, about the same age, were standing above the far side of the chute, and a third was on the ground, ready to swing the gate open. All were dusty from earlier attempts to ride the big calf.

The gate swung open and the white yearling spun and lunged into the open--twisting, kicking and turning. A grim expression on his face, the young rider hung on desperately with both hands. Just as the calf's front feet touched the ground at the end of the third leap, it ducked quickly to the left. The rider's weight shifted too far to the right and he tumbled into the dust. The calf seemed to sense where the boy was going to come down, and before the boy touched the ground the two rear hooves were striking out swiftly and sharply for the predetermined collision spot. As on three previous times that day, the hooves struck the rider--this time under the left arm. The force of the blow sent the youth rolling through the dust, cursing violently. The calf trotted to the far end of the corral and, ready to fight more if necessary, turned to face his tormentors.

Bill Thunder looked with admiration at the 18-month-old bull that had come out of the bucking chute eight times in one afternoon and was still unbeaten. The old Indian wasn't as impressed with the calf's ability to dispose of riders as he was with the amount of fight that remained. The boys hadn't even used a flank strap to ensure maximum bucking.

The calf was big, weighing close to a thousand pounds. Its mother was a Charlais and its father a Brahman, and the calf would nearly double its present weight before it fully matured. There was no brand on the white hide. Somehow, it had missed being captured, branded and castrated in the fall roundup a year ago--but now that it was caught it wouldn't be long until these matters were taken care of.

The boy that had been kicked was still holding his ribs when his companions went after the calf to get it in the bucking chute for one last ride. After the second ride, it had refused to be driven into the chute again, so the only way to get the animal in was to muscle it in with ropes, and that wasn't easy.

After one of the boys got a loop around the calf's neck, they proceeded to whip and pull until they got the rope around one of the stout chute posts. Then, taking up slack an inch or two at a time, they gradually worked the stubborn beast, fighting them every inch of the way, into the chute. Once into the end of the chute, with a pole behind its hind quarters, the only way to freedom for the calf was to move ahead.

As the boys wrestled the calf into the chute, Bill Thunder looked away from the struggling beast to the rugged Wasatch Mountains. He couldn't help but feel that some of the wild and free spirit of those mountains had been bred into the calf. Never had he seen a domestic animal with such spirit, with so much fight against domination by man.

Bill had originally come down to the corral to cheer on the bold youths who were attempting to ride this wild young bull. But after witnessing the fierce determination with which the yearling fought its riders, the old man found his sympathy switching from the boys to the calf.

As he watched the bull's unwavering determination to resist the boys, there was a growing sadness in Bill's old heart. This seemingly unconquerable spirit would soon be crushed through castration, soothed and lulled in the feedlot, then snuffed out at the slaughterhouse. The old man had no argument against the final destiny for which cattle were raised. He had killed and butchered his share during his lifetime. It was just that somehow this calf seemed different, like it had a greater spirit, like it was destined to something greater than merely vegetating in a feedlot.

The old man didn't know why he had these thoughts. It was just a feeling that grew in him as he watched the calf fight the boys.

The bucking gate flew open for the ninth time and the white bull leaped into the arena. This time at the end of the second leap it started to cut left, then ducked to the right instead, the rider plunging head over heels into the dirt, the striking hooves barely missing his face. The tired yearling trotted to the far end of the corral, ready to fight again.

The three bruised and dusty boys had had enough for one day and limped back to the bunkhouse, intentionally not leaving any hay or water for the young bull. Should they try to ride it again the next day, they wanted it to be weaker and slower.

It was late March and the sun was just disappearing behind the western hills. It didn't take long for the frosty evening air to coax Bill Thunder to leave his roost on the rail fence. Before turning away, however, he took a long last look at the young bull standing quietly at the far side of the corral.

Suddenly the sadness that the old man felt concerning the white calf was gone. He turned and strode confidently towards the bunkhouse, having reached a decision concerning the future of the animal in the corral.

Chapter 2

When Bill Thunder returned to the corral it was dark. He was driving his yellow and white 1973 Chevrolet pickup, which had wooden stock sides built from stud mill reject lumber. The truck moved slowly and quietly, lights off, as the old Indian carefully backed up to the loading chute.

He climbed the fence and disappeared into the darkness of the corral. He opened the gate leading to the chute and pickup, then the gate leading to the bucking chute, then walked quietly towards the white blur standing in darkness next to the corral fence.

As the old Indian drew near, he slapped his hat quietly against his leg. The calf trotted back across the corral, staying as far away from the entrance to the bucking chute as possible.

When the calf suddenly discovered the dark opening leading to the loading chute, he darted inside, thinking he had finally found a way to escape. Upon finding himself in the narrowness of the loading chute, he reversed his direction and started backing out, but it was too late. Bill Thunder had shoved a pole between the rails to block his exit. There was no way to go but forward into the back of the pickup, so that's where he went. Before the young bull could spin around and head back out again, the tailgate was closed.

The bull turned around again and again as Bill Thunder drove the pickup down the long driveway. When the old Indian reached the on-ramp to Interstate 15, he turned on the headlights and headed south.

About an hour later the truck left the interstate, heading west towards Hooper, Utah. A short time later, the young bull could hear heavy waves of water crashing against both sides of the narrow highway leading to Antelope Island, a rugged chunk of land approximately 20 miles long and three miles wide surrounded by the salty blue waters of the Great Salt Lake.

When Bill Thunder finally turned off the lights and engine, the truck was backed up to a high woven wire fence. Getting out of the truck, the old Indian reached under the seat for a bolt cutter. He walked to the back of the truck and cut an opening in the heavy wire that was big enough for the calf to jump through. When the tailgate was raised the calf didn't need any coaxing to leap to his freedom.

"May your medicine be strong, Medicine Bull," offered the old Indian as the young bull galloped away into the darkness. "Enjoy your freedom!"

After patching the hole in the fence with bailing wire, Bill Thunder headed home, confident the animal would enjoy complete freedom another year, perhaps even longer. The calf would be free to wander the rugged island with the wild buffalo that lived there, or even mix with the cattle that were sometimes allowed to winter on the island. The spring roundup had already been completed, so it would be another year before the young bull would be bothered by white men.

As Medicine Bull trotted away from the truck into the darkness, a strange feeling swelled up inside him. There was something different about this new land. It was wild, untamed. He had been raised on the open desert of northern Utah, but this new place was different.

The wild animals on the island were free to do as they pleased with very little interference from man.

The young bull sensed danger, freedom and a wildness he had never felt before. Wild, un- domesticated urges that had been buried deep inside for hundreds of generations began to push to the sur- face. It was as if he were galloping back in time, into the black jungles of India, to a time before his ancestors were captured and tamed by man.

The call of the wild was possessing his soul, as it sometimes does when domestic animals enter the wilds: like the gentle house cat that heads down the hunting trail into the woods never to return to man again; like the lazy, sleepy hog that wanders into the woods to become an alert, wary, and sometimes dangerous wild boar.

There is something about being alone and free in wild country that erases centuries of careful domestication. When the call of the wild wipes out that soothing sense of dependence upon man, the animal experiences a new intensity of spirit, a new awakening of the senses. It beomes more alert, more wary. Its muscles harden, its eyesight sharpens, it becomes aware of different scents carried on the breeze, and the very soul itself swells to new dimen- sions as the animal becomes a throwback, taking on the characteristics of its primitive forefathers.

And so it was with Medicine Bull as he wandered though the night, grazing occasionally but mostly ex- ploring, sniffing, looking, even listening to the night sounds.

Upon reaching the crest of a grassy ridge, quickly filling his mouth with the frosty yellow grass, the calf raised his head to look and listen, his drooping Brahman ears cocked forward to catch any sign that might signal danger. He didn't know yet who his enemies might be in this new land. His nostrils quivered, flaring to catch every new scent, and his eyes pierced the blackness of the night as best they could.

As the stars began to fade away into the grey dawn, Medicine Bull worked his way onto a rounded grassy ridge. He was grazing more contentedly now.

Suddenly, across a small ravine not more than a hundred yards away, Medicine Bull noticed about fifty buffalo grazing quietly in the early dawn. His instincts told him that even though these beasts looked different from any animal he had ever seen before, they were a kind of wild cattle, like him.

Eagerly, he galloped towards the buffalo. His instincts did not tell him of the mortal danger that awaited him.

At first sight of the white newcomer, the buffalo were startled, but they soon settled down to see what was going to happen as one of the huge herd bulls trotted out to challenge the eager yearling.

A short distance from the herd, the big bull stopped, lowered his massive head, and began pawing the partly frozen turf, snorting out long puffs of steamy breath. Every muscle in the 2500-pound carcass flexed with the excitement of possible battle with the young stranger.

The big bull made quick jabs at the air with his battle-seasoned horns. His huge neck and hump muscles gave those horns sufficient power not only to disembowel this newcomer, but to break the stranger's back and throw him ten feet into the air.

Unlike most domestic bulls that often seem quite unaware of the strength they possess, this old bull buffalo had tested his strength many times in battle and knew exactly what destructive power he had. He fully intended to put it to use on this 1000-pound yearling.

When Medicine Bull became aware of the angry buffalo in his path, he slowed to a walk, realizing that perhaps his welcome was not going to be a warm one. He continued walking, cautiously, towards the herd, until the big bull charged.

Medicine Bull spun back on his heels and headed

up the hill as hard as he could run. It didn't take long to realize that the old bull was gaining on him with every stride. For a moment or two, the yearling felt the despair of having an unavoidable appointment with violent destruction.

To stop and fight would be hopeless, and since it didn't appear he could outrun the attacking bull, there didn't seem to be any way out of the situation. Finally, when the charging buffalo was only a leap or two away, Medicine Bull, in a last effort, calling to the surface all the athletic ability inherited from his Brahman ancestors, darted quickly to the right. The charging buffalo turned right too, but not nearly as fast as Medicine Bull. As they circled back to the herd, the gap between them widened to 30 or 40 feet.

Enraged, the old bull galloped after the white yearling more ambitiously than before. When he was nearly upon the white newcomer for the second time, the young bull darted to the left, again widening the gap about the same as before. Realizing he wasn't going to catch the agile young bull, the buffalo stopped, pawed the ground a few more times, then returned to the herd.

At a safe distance, Medicine Bull watched the old buffalo. He realized the old fellow had meant business, had tried to kill him, and would probably try it again if the right opportunity came along.

Medicine Bull began to graze, lifting his head often to keep an eye on the buffalo around him. From deep inside, more of a feeling than a thought process, something told him he was going to like his new life with the wild buffalo on rugged Antelope Island.

Chapter 3

Medicine Bull soon found his place among the young bulls that roamed the periphery of the buffalo herd, being careful never to cross inside the imaginary circle around the nucleus of the herd where the cows, calves and established herd bulls belonged.

He learned that the buffalo were different in many ways from the cattle he had been raised with. The buffalo were more active and energetic. They ran, played and fought with much more energy and frequency than domestic cattle ever did.

As the weeks passed into months, Medicine Bull found himself constantly at play with the eager young buffalo, mostly those his own age and size. At first, he merely ran from them as he had from the old bull, but as his confidence grew and his native Brahman agility developed, he began to turn into them from time to time, bruising their ribs with his budding horns, which were more blunt than the buffalo horns and didn't have the deadly upward curl.

Most of the play took place during the early morning coolness or in the evening twilight. During the hot summer days, the buffalo rested in the shade of wooded draws, but as soon as the sun began to turn red as it approached the western horizon, the battle play of the young bulls resumed at full force.

In his almost daily battles with the young buffalo, the placid traits of domestication that man had bred into Medicine Bull over hundreds of generations were pushed further and further into the forgotten depths of his soul. At the same time, the wild traits of his an-

cient ancestors--the traits that had been suppressed for
many generations--were coaxed to the surface.

Medicine Bull found himself enjoying the battles
with the young buffalo more and more. And with increasing frequency it was Medicine Bull who started
the play, who charged fiercely upon a quietly grazing
young bull.

The men who managed the bison herd discovered
the white yearling soon after his arrival, but figuring
he could do no harm they left him alone, figuring they
could get him the next spring when the wintering cattle were rounded up.

The days became weeks, the weeks months. The
intense heat of the summer began to give way to the
cool fall breezes. One autumn night under a full moon,
Medicine Bull grazed eagerly following an afternoon
of exhausting play. He was on top of one of the highest
ridges, a cool breeze off the lake massaging his battle-
hardened muscles.

Unlike the daytime sun that caused drowsiness,
the cool fall breeze awakened a surge of strength and
confidence in the young bull that he had never known
before. As he looked down the hill at the grazing buffalo, the herd bulls were no longer as huge and
threatening as they had once been.

Every hardened muscle in Medicine Bull's young
body quivered with excitement as he realized that
someday he would engage in deadly battle with the
herd bulls to become one of them. He knew he wasn't
ready yet, and he didn't know when he would be
ready, but he knew that his time would come and this
realization thrilled him to the very core.

Medicine Bull became more fierce in his daily com-
bat with the young bulls. What had once been play
was now serious business to him. The mock battles
became bloody. The sharp horns of the buffalo began
finding their way through his white hide, leaving
bloody surface wounds that usually healed quickly,

leaving ugly black scars.

As the fighting grew more serious, demanding more strength and energy, the battles became less frequent. It took time to recoup spent strength and to allow wounds and bruises to heal. In early winter as the icy storms began to blow in off the lake, the battles became even less frequent as the buffalo sought shelter in the deep draws.

As winter approached, big trucks brought Hereford cattle to the island and turned them loose at the south end. But Medicine Bull did not mix with the cattle. He had found his place in the society of buffalo.

Medicine Bull was a ravenous grazer. It was as if he knew that his size and weight would be critical factors when he came to battle against the herd bulls. Going into winter, Medicine Bull weighed about 1300 pounds. By early spring he was pushing 1700 pounds, every ounce solid muscle.

It was early March when one of Medicine Bull's sparring companions, without warning, strolled in among the grazing cows as if he belonged there. The young buffalo had thrown down the challenge for which he had been preparing, and the challenge was instantly accepted by the nearest herd bull.

The two bulls faced each other, snorting, bawling and pawing dirt and gravel high into the air as if each was trying to scare the other off. Neither backed down.

As if on a given signal, they plunged into each other, going round and round, back and forth, crashing horns, pounding bodies, churning hooves, dust, dirt, blood and bellowing.

For the first minute or so the young challenger held his own, but soon the experience of the seasoned bull began to give the old fellow the advantage and the young bull was doing most of the backing away. Finally, the challenger got caught sideways with a terrible thrust and went down.

Not about to give up his advantage, the seasoned veteran moved in on his downed opponent, goring and butting with all the ferocity he could muster. The young one, spinning and rolling, was trying desperately to get back on his feet, realizing that not only the outcome of the battle, but his very life, was at stake.

The battle pushed close to where Medicine Bull was watching. Filled with the excitement of real battle, he eyed the unguarded side of the seasoned herd bull as it brutally unleashed its fury on the desperate young bull. Medicine Bull could contain himself no longer.

Releasing all his pent-up strength into a sudden charge, the white bull smashed into the side of the unsuspecting old bull, bowling him over on his side. Medicine Bull followed up, butting and goring with all his might, but the battle-wary old fellow was soon on his feet returning the fight with all his heart.

By this time the young bull was also back on his feet, joining Medicine Bull. Together they began to get the best of the old warrior. In their youthful excitement, however, they didn't realize their two-on-one advantage was a violation of herd law.

The two young bulls didn't see the second herd bull charging in to even the odds until it was too late. Medicine Bull barely saw the newcomer in time to spin around enough to avoid a direct broadside assault, which could easily have been fatal. As it was, the charging bull smashed shoulder to shoulder into Medicine Bull, at the same time goring him viciously. The horn pushed between the ribs, tearing through skin, flesh and lung before Medicine Bull could twist away.

The newcomer to the fight was turning in for another lunge when Medicine Bull's young companion hit him in the hind quarter. In the meantime, the first herd bull had recovered and with a loud bellow was charging back into the fight.

Medicine Bull and his companion had had enough and were retreating at a full gallop down the valley. The herd bulls followed them only a little way before stopping to bellow out a few warning threats to the retreating youngsters and paw dirt into the air. Then the old fellows proudly returned to the herd.

Medicine Bull hadn't run far when his mouth filled with blood. He was suddenly overcome with sickness and nausea, and an almost irresistible force was urging him to lie down, his strength almost gone. He resisted the urge, instinctively knowing that once he was down he might not be able to get up for a long time, leaving him to the mercy of the herd bulls.

He headed for a thick patch of willows below one of the mountain springs and barely made it into the green jungle before collapsing and coughing up blood. His muscles were screaming for more oxygen, which his lungs were unable to provide, but as he lay panting in the willows, the good lung gradually began to make up the deficiency. Still, it was several days before Medicine Bull had the strength to stand again, and several weeks before he had the strength to leave the willows and again roam the hillsides.

Even though the gored lung almost killed Medicine Bull, it was lucky for him that the injury occurred when it did, because it was only two days later when the spring roundup of the wintering cattle began. The men who had been keeping an eye on the wintering cattle had noticed the white bull and had intended to pick him up in the spring drive, but as they brought the white-faced cattle out of the hills, the young white bull could not be found. Riders came close to him several times, yelling and beating the brush, but he remained perfectly still in his hiding place, too weak to get up and run.

It wasn't until April when the warm spring sun began drying up the June grass that the men who

managed the island again noticed the young white bull
running with the buffalo. Several riders were sent out
to try and drive him into the corrals, but they found
him as hard to manage as the rankest buffalo bulls and
they gave up. It was decided to let the white bull stay
with the buffalo for another season.

By the time summer arrived, Medicine Bull had his
full strength back and was again engaging in mock
battles with his friends. Because of the goring he was
more cautious now and began to develop his own
fighting style, somewhat different than that of the buffalo.

His horns were different, blunt and broad and
about six inches long, pointing straight out to the side
instead of curving up like those of his companions.

Instead of using the straight-ahead attack of his
companions, Medicine Bull found that if he went in at
an angle he could effectively thrust his head sideways
into an opponent's shoulder or side and when the opponent pulled away, he could spin around and blast
out with both hind feet, something the buffalo seldom
did.

Because of the injury, Medicine Bull had gained
plenty of respect for buffalo horns and now found
himself developing his instinctive Brahman athletic
ability to the utmost--jabbing, spinning, kicking, and
at all times keeping out of range of his opponents'
horns.

With each battle, Medicine Bull found himself
deviating more and more from the standard buffalo
fighting style, and the more he changed the more successful he became. The goring from the big herd bull,
however, wasn't quickly forgotten, and as the summer months passed, Medicine Bull was careful to keep
a safe distance between himself and the big bulls.

But with the coming of fall and the cool refreshing
breezes from the lake, memories of the goring began
to fade, and Medicine Bull found himself grazing

across the invisible barrier separating the young bulls from the main herd.

Finally, on a sunny fall afternoon his boldness was challenged. Medicine Bull had been waiting for this day for a long time. He was in his prime now, weighing over 2,000 pounds. He was three years old and over half his life had been lived on the wild shores of Antelope Island with the buffalo. He had developed a fighting style all his own, and he was now ready to test it against even the most aggressive of the herd bulls.

He grazed in among the cows and calves and wasn't there long before a huge bull trotted to within 20 yards, stopped, pawed chunks of sod into the air, and bellowed out a challenge to Medicine Bull, who seemed to ignore the old fellow.

The young bull kept his nose in the grass as if he were still grazing, but he had forgotten the grass and was intently watching the old bull preparing to attack. Medicine Bull was standing sideways, offering a broadside target for the angry buffalo, who soon broke into a vicious charge.

Medicine Bull kept his nose in the grass until the bull was nearly upon him, then lunged forward as if caught by surprise. The old buffalo changed its direction in anticipation of the forward lunge. At the last instant, Medicine Bull changed direction and spun to the rear. The buffalo's horns found nothing but air, and the old fellow was nearly knocked off his feet as Medicine Bull let loose a striking blow with both hind feet into his opponent's belly. As the herd bull spun around, the same two feet caught him again, square in the side of the neck, stopping him dead in his tracks. The buffalo backed off a moment to take a better look at his young opponent.

When the second charge came, the attacker was bellowing out his rage louder than ever. Again Medicine Bull faked to the side, this time thrusting a blunt horn into the buffalo's ribs, then spinning around and planting both hind feet squarely into the exposed shoulder.

The battle was over almost as quickly as it had begun. The buffalo, puffing from his exertions, saliva drooling from his half-open mouth, resumed his grazing. Medicine Bull had held his own. He had won the first important battle.

Over the next few weeks the white bull battled three or four of the other herd bulls. The results were always the same. By mid-November he was a full-fledged member of the main herd, allowed to wander at will among the cows and calves. And, of course, one of his main duties was to keep the young bulls away.

For Medicine Bull the rest of the winter was uneventful but happy. He was respected by the mighty herd bulls, feared by the young bulls, admired by the cows, and the calves loved to race playfully about him. He was free to do as he pleased. He was fulfilled, satisfied and happy. But it was all destined to end.

Chapter 4

In March, Medicine Bull was herded into the roundup corrals along with the wintering cattle and several of the buffalo. After some cutting and selecting he was herded into the pen with the animals that were to be shipped to the local livestock sale.

About a week later, Medicine Bull and one of the buffalo bulls were loaded into the back of a one-ton truck with a covered stock rack. The truck headed south to Interstate 80, east to the I-15 interchange, then south again.

Two hours later the truck left the freeway and a few minutes later backed up to a wooden chute. The tailgate was hoisted and the two bulls charged down the ramp into a high-fenced corral. It felt good to Medicine Bull to be on the ground again. He wouldn't have felt so good, however, had he been able to understand the meaning of the words on the big sign. Spanish Fork Packing Company. He was in the holding corral of a slaughterhouse.

Jerry Larsen had gone to Antelope Island to pick up a buffalo the hospital guild had purchased for an upcoming barbecue. Jerry was a member of the guild and had helped organize the barbecue to raise funds to help pay for an addition to the nearby Payson Hospital.

While picking up the buffalo at the island, one of the livestock managers asked Jerry if he would take the white bull too. They agreed on a price, and Medicine Bull was loaded into the truck with the buffalo. Whereas the buffalo was going to be barbecued to raise money for a hospital, Medicine Bull was going to be made into hamburger and frankfurters. In fact, execution was scheduled for the very next morning.

That night while the two bulls were chewing on flakes of green alfalfa hay, oblivious to the fact that by the next night their carcasses were scheduled to be hanging upside down in the meat cooler, Jerry attended a meeting of the hospital guild to work out the final details for the barbecue, which was only a week away.

A car dealer by the name of Jim Bird was the ticket chairman, and when he gave the report on ticket sales, a spirit of gloom descended upon the group. Sales were way below expectations. In fact, there hadn't even been enough tickets sold to pay for the buffalo. Bird guessed that maybe it was a little too early in the season. People couldn't count on warm weather, so they didn't buy tickets.

"We've got to come up with a gimmick," said Bird, "something besides food, something that'll make people want to come to the fairgrounds next Saturday, regardless of the weather. Anybody have any ideas?"

The room was silent for a few minutes as everyone strained in fruitless thought.

"How about a bullfight?" suggested Jerry, not really serious about the idea but figuring any suggestion would be better than none. Perhaps it would start the ball rolling, would lead to a good idea. Someone asked him to elaborate.

"I was just thinking about a rank old bull I bought at Antelope Island when I was up there to pick up the buffalo. People told me this bull had been raised on the refuge with the buffalo. No one knows how he got there, but he's the wildest-looking bull I've ever seen, and I've seen plenty.

"If you turned him in an arena with some of our local cowboys," he continued, "he would put on a pretty good show. You've got to see him to appreciate him. He's pure white and covered with black scars from fighting them buffalo. He weighs more than a ton, and walks with the agility and lightness of a cat. There's no brand on him. As far as I know, he's never been caught before, never had a rope on him, and maybe he's never even been touched by a human being. As I said, he's the wildest-looking critter you'll ever lay your eyes on."

"Rather than a bullfight," suggested Bird with more enthusiasm than he had felt in a long time, "I'll put up five hundred dollars for the first cowboy who can ride that bull for eight seconds."

The members of the guild sat up in their chairs. The idea was getting very interesting.

"There's a lot of cowboys at this end of the valley," continued Bird. "A good share of them think they're pretty good bull riders, and they have plenty of friends who would want to watch them prove it. We'll draw their names out of a hat in the order they're to ride. The first man to stay on for eight seconds gets the five hundred bucks."

"Hey, I think this idea has some real possibilities," said Scott Hunter, a local radio personality. He raised his hand to his mouth, then said as if making an announcement into a microphone, "Attention, ladies and gentlemen, Bird Motors is offering five hundred dollars--that's right, five hundred dollars--to the first cowboy who can ride Moby Dick for eight seconds....

"Why is Bird so generous? Well, he isn't. He doesn't think anyone can ride this critter. You see, Moby Dick is not a fish, but a bull, fresh from the wild back country of Antelope Island, where he was raised with the wild buffalo. He's every bit as mean and untamed as his wild companions. He's never been ridden before, and Bird Motors is betting five hundred dollars that he won't be ridden next Saturday, either. Come to the buffalo barbecue Saturday and see if there's a Utah Valley cowboy good enough to ride

Moby Dick. If you know a cowboy that could use an extra five hundred dollars, have him call this station for more information.... By the way, Payson Hospital is offering free patch-up and repair for any cowboy that can't last the full eight seconds...."

The idea mushroomed into reality and Medicine Bull's appointment with the slaughtering crew was postponed for a week so he could help promote the buffalo barbecue for the Payson Hospital Guild.

The wild bull riding idea paid off. Over two thousand people migrated to the fairgrounds that Saturday afternoon, stuffing themselves with thousands of buffalo sandwiches at two dollars each and washing them down with root beer and apple cider at 75 cents a cup. By 2 p.m. everyone had crowded into the grandstands, waiting for the bull riding to begin.

Medicine Bull had no idea what was going on until he was hazed down the alley into the bucking chutes. Gradually, unpleasant memories of his day with the Indian boys on the Bear River ranch began to return and the adrenalin surged through his veins.

He knew what he had to do when the braided rigging fell across his muscular shoulders. Medicine Bull tried to shake the rope free, but couldn't. Then he just stood still, waiting to explode. He didn't have long to wait.

As soon as Medicine Bull felt the cowboy's weight on his back, he began leaping and twisting in the confines of the chute. The cowboy couldn't get firmly seated. The gate remained closed. Finally, in one of Medicine Bull's upward lunges, the cowboy's knee was slammed against the bottom edge of one of the side boards. He grunted in pain as ligaments were torn. The gate remained closed, and cowboy number one climbed to safety above the chute, relinquishing his chance at the five hundred dollars.

The second cowboy was luckier than the first in

that he finally got his seating and was able to signal the gate keeper. When the gate began to open, Medicine Bull froze for an instant, trying to comprehend what was happening, then lunged towards the opening with all his strength.

The bull's first leap was too ambitious. When his front feet touched down, his hindquarters were too high and moving forward with too much momentum, pushing him into a full sommersault. The bull landed on his back, while the desperate cowboy managed to wiggle to one side just in time to avoid being crushed beneath the bull's body. Both instantly scrambled to their feet, but before the cowboy could scramble to safety, Medicine Bull caught him between the shoulder blades with a hind foot and sent the hapless young man sprawling face down in the dirt.

As the bull spun around to do more damage to the cowboy, a funny-looking little man with a painted face and baggy pants ran between the animal and the cowboy and began teasing Medicine Bull with a red umbrella. The bull quickly forgot the cowboy and lunged at the clown. His horns found nothing but air as he charged past. When he turned to face the clown a second time, Medicine Bull realized the clown had tricked him as he had tricked the buffalo.

A little smarter, the bull lunged again, but this time as he rushed by, he lashed out with his hind feet. A score. As he spun around and was heading in to get the clown again, the little fellow scampered into a barrel. Medicine Bull hit the barrel several times but the clown wouldn't come out.

Two men on horses hazed the bull into a corral and in a minute he found himself back in one of the bucking chutes. This time he had to wait a little longer, because the next two riders decided at the last minute to pass on the opportunity to win five hundred dollars, and the next man in line had to be found.

The second time out of the chute, Medicine Bull

leaped high into the air, coming down with his front legs at an angle, enabling him to dart sharply to the left. As the rider hit the ground, Medicine Bull caught him in the ribs with a swift kick, then chased the more careful clown over the fence.

By the time the wary hazers had maneuvered the white bull back into the chute for the third ride of the day, there was no one to ride him. There were plenty of cowboys standing around, and most of them had ridden bulls before, but none felt inclined to try Medicine Bull, not after what he had done to the first riders.

The crowd began to grow restless. They had paid money to watch some wild bull riding and they hadn't received their money's worth, not yet.

Chapter 5

Sitting near the back of the crowd, elbows on knees, was Byron Horn. He was a professional bull rider, 20 years old. He was from Spanish Fork, had started riding bulls in high school rodeo competition, and had done so well--first place in the Utah high school rodeo championships his senior year--that he went professional right out of high school.

He won a little over $3,000 in prize money the first season, traveling to rodeos throughout the Intermountain Region. The second season was a lot better, with over $8,000 in winnings. Now, at the beginning of his third season, his goal was to reach the national finals in Oklahoma City in November, when the top 15 money winners in each rodeo event were invited to compete in the world championships.

"Why don't you ride him?" asked the red-haired girl sitting next to him, her arm in his. "Not very many bulls can throw you. Don't you think you can do it?"

"I'm not sure," responded Byron thoughtfully, removing his hat and looking inside but not seeing anything. "He's one of the rankest bulls I've ever seen. It would be stupid for me to try. Even if I did it, the ride wouldn't count towards the world championships. And if I failed and got hurt, I could be out for the season. It's a no-win situation."

"I have just received word," boomed the announcer with increased enthusiasm, "that Byron Horn is in the stands. Many of you already know that Byron

is probably the best bull rider this valley has ever produced. There's a good chance he'll be competing in
the rodeo world championships in Oklahoma next
fall. Come on down, Byron, and ride this bull. Show
us how it's done. Byron Horn, are you here?''

Byron placed his hat back on his head and slouch-
ed low in his seat, not wanting to be noticed. He didn't
want to tackle that bull. Someone a few rows back,
however, spotted the young cowboy.

"Here he is!" shouted the spectator. Everyone
turned to look at Byron.

"Come on, son," said another man. "Show us you
can ride that bull."

When Byron shook his head, giving a negative
response, the crowd began to chant, "We want Horn,
we want Horn...."

Byron continued to shake his head, a half-
embarrassed smile on his face.

His girlfriend began to push too. "Oh Byron.
You've ridden a hundred bulls, some tougher than
that one, I'm sure. Why not this one?"

The young cowboy didn't respond, just sat there
looking at his boots. The crowd continued to chant,
the red-haired girl to nag.

Finally Byron stood up. The crowd cheered wildly.
He started down the wooden steps towards the arena.
Thousands of eyes were glued to the back of his sun-
browned muscular neck, broad shoulders, narrow
hips, well-developed legs, powerful arms and rugged
hands.

Byron wasn't very tall, 5'10" or 5'11", about 170
pounds, just right for a bull rider. No one could question his natural athletic ability as they watched his liquid movements when he descended the stairs and
hurdled the fence. Everything about him was graceful
and strong, even his face, with the firm lines of his
jaw, high cheekbones, narrow lips, and steel-blue
eyes, weather wrinkled at the corners. The hair on his

head was curly and blond, but most of it was hidden beneath his drooping cowboy hat, the kind popular among bull riders and high school kids. He was the epitome of the male athlete, the kind of man a Michelangelo would select as a model when sculpting a David.

Byron Horn had been an excellent athlete all his life and had excelled in football in high school. In fact, he had done so well that he had received three offers for full-ride football scholarships.

Byron was a running back, and a good one. Still, he had turned down the scholarships, against the advice of friends, relatives and teachers.

When asked why he turned down a promising football career to become a bull rider, he was hard-pressed to give an answer. He enjoyed football very much, but though some people took it very seriously, it was only a game to Byron and would never be anything more.

Bull riding was different. A mistake by a rider could cost him a lot more than a few points on a scoreboard--maybe a broken back, a smashed pelvis or a gored lung. To a 2,000-pound Brahman, bull riding was not a game. The animal had no rules to restrict or civilize him. He could smash a rider's knee against a chute, kick him in the groin, gore him in the guts, or just jump on his chest with both front feet, all 2,000 pounds of him. Sure, there were injuries in football, but they were accidents or against the rules. Not so in bull riding. If a bull killed or maimed a rider, it was because that is exactly what the bull was trying to do, and he wouldn't feel bad about it at all. He would do it again if he could.

Byron sometimes thought of himself as an adrenalin addict, and football just couldn't make it flow, not like bull riding. But now as he walked across the arena towards the chute where the white bull was waiting restlessly for him, the young bull rider could feel the adrenalin surging through his body with a violence that made every muscle throb hot with anticipation of the approaching battle.

Byron forgot the crowd, his girlfriend, the announcer, the five hundred dollars. He was thinking of one thing--that white animal in the bucking chute and how it had behaved its first two times out. The sharp changes in direction, from left to right--that's what he'd have to watch for. And if he managed to stay on for the required eight seconds, then what. Getting off would be a problem because as soon as his feet hit the ground, possibly before, the bull would be after him, kicking and goring. The adrenalin was flowing because Byron knew that what he was about to do was not sport, but serious battle where not only serious injury, but perhaps even his life, was at stake.

Byron borrowed a bull-riding rigging from one of the cowboys behind the chute and with the cowboy's help secured it to Medicine Bull. The bull was quieter as Byron lowered himself onto the white back. It wasn't that the bull was getting tired or tame or more subdued. He was learning the rules, that the time to get rid of the rider was after the gate opened, not before.

Byron wrapped the rigging end around his gloved left hand several times to ensure a firm grip. His legs were squeezing firmly against the muscled sides of the bull. With his right hand he shoved his hat down over his ears and signaled for the gate to open.

Byron had hoped that, this being the bull's third time out of the chute, the animal might be a little weary. Such was not the case as Medicine Bull exploded into the opening gate with such fury that the gate man was knocked down.

As Medicine Bull's front feet hit the ground at the end of his first lunge, he dodged quickly to the left, expecting the rider to tumble right, but Byron remained in position. With even more fury the bull lunged again, this time dodging right, expecting the rider to tumble left. Again Byron stayed with the animal. A few additional bucks with a lot of angry twisting and shaking, and still the rider remained. Three and one-half seconds had elapsed since the gate had opened.

Leaping forward like a racehorse breaking from the starting gate, Medicine Bull gathered momentum for a high, long, twisting leap. Byron was lying almost flat back, spurs locked firmly against the bull's shoulders.

This time, instead of veering to the left or right as Byron expected, Medicine Bull landed stiff-legged and was leaping straight back the instant his front feet hit the ground.

Byron did a complete sommersault over the bull's head and was knocked senseless for an instant as his entire body slammed flat against the ground. Seeing his new technique had worked, Medicine Bull immediately changed directions again, lunging towards the hapless cowboy. Instead of using his horns, the bull leaped into the air, coming down with both front feet on the youth's body, smashing ribs, fracturing the pelvis, and bruising liver, lungs, intestines and everything else in the vicinity.

Before Medicine Bull could turn around to finish his work, the clown raced past his nose. The bull lunged after him and soon found a gate closing behind him just as the clown scampered over a fence.

Looking back through the gate, Medicine Bull saw the flashing red lights of the ambulance as it pulled alongside the unconscious bull rider. As the bull watched the strange happenings, he had no idea that he would run into that cowboy again someday.

As Medicine Bull watched the flashing lights, he had no way of knowing that the bold behavior that had nearly killed the young cowboy had saved himself from the slaughterhouse. Already, word of his exploits was spreading by the owners of several rodeo bucking strings. By the end of the day, when doctors would still be working hard to patch up Byron Horn, the price on Medicine Bull's head as a bucking bull would be many times his value as a hamburger and frankfurter bull.

Chapter 6

It was late September when Byron's horse finished drinking its fill of the green mossy water of Maple Lake. It wasn't really a lake as much as a big watering hole or a small pond. There were no fish in it, but plenty of pollywogs and frogs. Located at the head of a sweeping alpine valley just north of Spanish Fork Peak, the little lake was a favorite watering hole for deer and elk, and Byron noticed plenty of fresh tracks in the soft mud at the water's edge.

The trail forked at the lake and Byron tried to decide whether to take the left fork over the ridge and down into the Little Diamond drainage or follow the main trail past the peak south towards Wind Rock Ridge. He decided on the latter, figuring there would be less chance of running into other people. Except during hunting season, very few people ventured into this rugged region of the Wasatch Range.

Three hours earlier Byron had left his pickup and horse trailer near the end of the road in Maple Canyon. He was traveling light. Saddlebags, thermal blanket, yellow rain slicker, picket rope and hatchet were the only camping items attached to his roping saddle. Inside the saddlebags were dehydrated soup mixes, instant cocoa mix, instant orange drink, granola bars, extra horseshoes and nails, string, salt, a spoon, an aluminum pan, and a U.S. Forest Service trail map. Byron prided himself on being able to take off into the wilderness for a week or two at a time with only five or six pounds of food in his saddlebags. Of course, he supplemented his prepared food with wild berries and an occasional fat porcupine or prairie chicken.

Byron was riding Ginger, a seven-year-old buckskin quarter horse gelding. The well-muscled animal stood 15 hands tall and weighed about 1,000 pounds. He was quick and aggressive in the roping arena, sure-footed and level-headed in the mountains.

After leaving the truck and trailer at the bottom of the canyon, Byron headed up the well-maintained trail into the heart of the Maple Mountain back country. He was in no hurry to go any place in particular. He just wanted to be alone for a week so he could sort out some of the problems that had been bothering him lately. His general plan was to follow the trail to the lake, then wander through the remote high-mountain valleys.

He had spent the beginning of the summer in the hospital, mending from that disastrous bull ride. He had had a fractured pelvis, numerous broken ribs, and badly bruised internal organs--injuries given him by the wild white bull raised with the buffalo on Antelope Island.

After getting out of the hospital, Byron had spent the rest of the summer recuperating at the family farm near the mouth of Spanish Fork Canyon. Before the injury he had been anticipating a successful summer of bull riding. Based on his record of the previous two summers, it had looked like he had a good chance at making the world championships in Oklahoma City, but the injuries had smashed those hopes, at least for the current year. Still, the doctors assured him he would be as strong as ever the next season.

But now, as Byron rode up the rocky trail, he didn't know if there was going to be another season for him. He was seriously questioning his life-long ambition to become a world champion bull rider. His parents, who at one time encouraged and cheered him on, had changed their opinion of bull riding. To them, it was now a foolhardy way to make a living. He was 21 and should be settling down, selecting a life-long profession, perhaps continuing his schooling, and beginning to raise a family. This reasoning made sense, but still, Byron had to make up his own mind.

What bothered him more than his parents' logic were the questions of his friends, especially Kent, who was studying liberal arts at the University of Utah in Salt Lake City.

"What's so great about riding bulls?" Kent had asked while visiting Byron at the hospital. "What does it prove? Does it make the world a better place? Does it reduce the risk of nuclear war? Does bull riding make the world cleaner, more peaceful, or more productive? Why don't you do something important, something that will make a difference? Get into politics or help clean up the environment--become an investigative reporter. Do something that has some substance, some value--and that's not staying on a bull's back for eight seconds."

Byron hadn't answered the questions. He couldn't put into words the value of being able to swallow fear as you climbed on top of a chute to look down upon a new bull you were going to try to ride. There were always the young cowboys around who searched your face for any sign of fear, seeking comfort in knowing they were not alone in the fear they felt. But you never gave them such satisfaction. No matter how afraid you were, you always acted as if riding a bull was as easy as galloping a gentle saddle horse. Byron believed that if the cowboys started talking openly about their bull riding fears, soon there wouldn't be anyone left to ride the bulls.

And then there was the ride. Fear vanished with the opening of the gate. The superhuman efforts to keep your seat--the thrills, pain, surprises--no more time for fear. Trying to outthink the bull, guess what he would do next and be ready. Feeling the muscles in your legs, arms and back strain to maximum strength and beyond. And then that unexplainable feeling when the whistle sounded and you were still in command of your bull.

What value is there in such experiences? Was it worth the risk, the injury, the worry, the pain? Just because you enjoyed doing it, did that make it worth doing?

Byron was bothered by his other friends too, the non-idealistic ones--the ones out for a good time--those who spent a lot of time watching television, cruising Main Street on Saturday nights, drinking and chasing women. Some of these friends, mostly former high school buddies, rode bulls too, but only once a year, at fair time. After the fair was over they had enough bull riding experiences to bask in for another year and to justify hanging riggings, ropes and bells on the gun racks of their pickups for all to see. Generally, there was enough excitement in one bull ride to last most of these friends an entire year.

But to get on three or four bulls a week for an entire season was more than these friends could comprehend. The price to pay to become a champion was beyond their grasp. And nobody understood the price that had to be paid better than Byron.

It's one thing to get on a bull with a gang of friends around shouting encouragement to you, your girlfriend waiting breathlessly in the stands, and about another hundred people you know looking on in anxious anticipation, cheering for you.

But it's another matter to drive all night, arriving in a strange town, tired, dirty and hungry fifteen minutes before you are scheduled to ride a strange bull you know nothing about. There are no familiar faces to offer a smile of encouragement, and when the gate opens, the crowd is just as likely to cheer for the bull as for you. And to be hurt in such a town, for strangers to take you to an unfamiliar hospital. No friends. No relatives. That's an awful experience and makes one wonder if bull riding is really worth the price.

These were the thoughts that were troubling Byron Horn as he turned away from Maple Lake and headed up the rocky trail towards Spanish Fork Peak.

He had been on the trail about an hour and probably wouldn't have noticed how the little trail leading off into a side canyon had been covered with rocks and sticks had his horse not tried to follow it anyway.

Just as he realized he was off the main trail and was turning the horse back, he spotted something unusual- -a freshly cut stump end. He wondered why anyone would go to the trouble of cutting down a green tree in such a remote place. The trunk of the tree was gone, but the branches were strewn across the trail.

Byron stopped his horse and looked at the stump for a minute. Why would anyone want to cover up the trail? He removed the Forest Service map from his saddlebag. The little trail was not on it. He couldn't help but wonder where it led to and why anyone would want to cover it up. There were no signs of use on the little trail, no old horse droppings or even any motor bike tracks. Why would someone want to hide the trail?

Byron's first thought was that perhaps this was a favorite hunting spot for someone who wanted to keep his secret place private. Perhaps a prospector had made a discovery and was working mine without attempting to go through all the Forest Service red tape.

Byron pulled his horse around and started riding back to the main trail. But he couldn't keep his mind off the sawed stump end and what was now the mystery of Maple Mountain. The further he rode the more curious he became as to why someone wanted to keep people out of the little canyon where the trail led.

For the first time in months, Byron was worrying about something besides bull riding. It was a pleasant change. He stopped the horse.

There was no hurry to get home, and there was no predetermined course he had to follow. He had plenty of food. He turned the horse around again, deciding to find out why someone was covering up the little trail.

Chapter 7

Byron followed the little trail into a wooded draw, then dismounted, leading his horse along the sidehill above the trail where he could have a better view of the little valley. He scanned the bottom of the draw as well as the hillsides for unnatural earth formations that would indicate possible mining. There were none. He scanned the groves of pine, cedar and aspen for signs of abundant game, evidence that he was entering someone's favorite hunting ground. It seemed there were less game signs than in the other places he had been that day.

But there was plenty of majestic scenery--jagged mountain peaks cutting into a deep blue Utah sky. A white crystalline stream snaked and writhed among boulders and logs at the bottom of the draw. The thick green fur and cedar forests and green meadows filled in the smooth places between the jagged ridges and cliffs.

An occasional patch of stained snow in a high shaded pocket reminded Byron that the summer richness of this high country was but a temporary condition that must be enjoyed quickly and deeply before it disappeared before the icy whiteness of winter.

Byron loved the rugged, untouched look of the mountain valleys. He couldn't explain why, but it inspired feelings of confidence and strength. He was nothing but a tiny dot on an endless range of granite mountains, sprawling forests and sparkling streams. Still, there was something in the majesty of the mountains that made him feel like a lot more than a tiny dot.

Being in the middle of God's most beautiful creations awakened grand feelings, made Byron feel like there was no limit to what he could accomplish.

His personal problems and worries dwindled to insignificance next to the grandeur of the granite peaks. And with that dwindling, the latent confidence and strength from deep inside welled to the surface-- making him feel fearless, bold and happy--ready to return home and become the greatest bull rider in the world, even a rich businessman or a successful rancher. Any goal or dream seemed within his grasp.

Byron had felt this way before, but knew that when he returned to civilized society, mingling with other people, the dreams of the mountains somehow became tainted, muddied, more distant, less real. Fears and insecurities grew, confidence waned.

He wondered if it were possible to keep and maintain permanently the confidence he felt in the mountains. If he could do that, life would be better. He would try. He would find a way.

Byron took a deep breath of the cool mountain air. It was good to be alone in the mountains.

At least he thought he was alone, until he heard a muffled noise, almost like a human voice, carried on the breeze from somewhere down the draw. Still leading his horse, Byron angled in the direction of the strange sound, thinking the wind was probably responsible for the unusual noise.

Byron hadn't gone far, however, when he realized he was hearing a human voice--a strong, loud, masculine voice shouting commands.

Upon reaching the foot of a rocky overhang, beyond which the horse could not go, Byron tied the animal to a cedar stump and began working his way around a rocky ledge. He hadn't gone far when he spotted a big flat rock above him. He was sure that's where the noise was coming from. He started climbing.

He was close enough now to begin understanding the words that were being shouted.

"Move, I said," the voice boomed. "I command you to move. Now! What are you waiting for?" The voice was deep and very forceful.

Byron had no idea what was happening on the flat rock. The person or thing being commanded to move didn't seem to be responding to the command. At least, Byron could hear no response. He continued to climb, as quietly as possible.

He slowed upon approaching the top of the rock. He had no idea what was going on, and he began to fear that he might be butting into someone's private business. Carefully, Byron peeked over the top of the big rock.

Not more than 30 feet away stood a fierce-looking man. He was little, maybe 140 or 150 pounds, with a fiery red beard that had a rebellious and unkempt look to it, like it hadn't been combed or trimmed in months.

The cold fire in the little man's blue eyes was focused on something across the canyon. He stood firmly in the center of the rock, feet slightly apart, right arm raised to the square like he was taking an oath. His left hand was curled into a threatening fist about a foot in front of his face.

"Look," he resumed shouting. "I'm not going to stand here and shout all day. I said move. Do it. Now. I don't care if you go left. I don't care if you go right. I don't care if you go forwards, backwards, up or down. Just move. I command it."

Byron looked about for any hint of who or what the man might be speaking to, but there was nothing, just the mountains and forests. In front of the little man the rock dropped sharply off and there was nothing but open space and the vast cavity of the canyon.

Byron shrugged his shoulders and said, "I don't know who you are shouting at, but it looks to me like he's already moved."

He then climbed into full view on top of the rock as the little man spun around to face the newcomer, his face more crimson than his beard.

"Who are you?" demanded the little man.

"Byron Horn. Who are you?"

"What are you doing here?"

"Heard you yelling. Thought you might need some help."

The two just stared at each other for a moment.

"What's all the shouting about?" asked Byron, breaking the silence.

The little man continued to stare, the crimson gradually draining from his face.

"What are you doing in this canyon?" asked the little man as if he owned the mountain.

"Someone tried to cover the trail. Thought I'd just come down here and find out why. Was it you?"

The little man didn't respond, standing in a half crouch, eyeing Byron. The man wore black leather hiking boots with cleated soles, a red wool shirt, and faded denim trousers held high with wide black suspenders.

"How did you get in here?" asked Byron, breaking the silence. "The trail didn't show any sign of anyone else coming down here. Figured I was the first, until I heard you shouting."

Instead of responding, the little man suddenly spun around, scampered over the far side of the rock and out of sight. Instinctively, Byron darted after him.

Chapter 8

Like a mountain goat, the red-haired man leaped from rock to rock as he worked his way across the mountain. Wearing leather-soled cowboy boots, Byron foolishly tried to keep up. He shouldn't have.

Byron's left boot slipped on the side of a big rock and he hit hard on his right knee. Lurching back from the pain, he lost his balance, tumbling into a narrow crevice where he became wedged between two smooth pieces of rock.

Byron cursed his bad luck. He tried to wiggle free, but the more he moved the tighter he became wedged between the two rocks. Realizing the helplessness of his situation, he started yelling for help, hoping the wild man wasn't too far away by now to hear him.

Like a huge vise, the stone walls angled in against Byron's hips and he soon forgot the pain in his knee. The harder he struggled, the tighter he became wedged in the stone trap. He called for help, again and again.

Byron scolded himself for being foolish enough to try to follow the little man. He hadn't been very smart trying to run across the rocks in cowboy boots. He realized it was late afternoon and would soon be dark. He didn't like the idea of spending a chilly night stuck between two slabs of hard, cold rock, knowing a crazy man was lurking about.

"You really do need help," said a voice so close that as Byron jerked his head up he banged it hard against the rock face. A red-haired face was looking down at him from the top of the crevice. It was the man he had been chasing.

"Hang on just a minute more, and I'll be back with something to get you out," said the little man before he disappeared.

A few minutes later he returned with a sapling, about two inches in diameter. He trimmed the branches off with his knife, then lowered the small end to Byron, who grabbed it firmly with both hands.

The wild man tried to pull the trapped cowboy to freedom, but the latter was wedged too tightly between the rocks, and all the tugging and pulling didn't seem to do any good. If anything, Byron only became more tightly wedged between the two rocks.

Finally the wild man threw the sapling aside and disappeared a second time. After what seemed a long time to Byron, the little man returned, dragging a half-rotten log, which he stuffed into the crevice a few feet away from Byron. He disappeared again, this time returning with a long pole he shoved over the top of the rotten log and under Byron's dangling feet.

Pushing down on one end of the pole gave the little man the leverage he needed. Byron braced his legs firmly against his end of the lever as it pushed upwards against the bottoms of his feet.

At first Byron didn't move, but as the force of the lever increased and as he squirmed between the rocks, he gradually felt the rock surfaces begin to grind against clothing, skin and bone in the tight places as his body was forced upward to where there was more room to move.

Byron soon had enough room to start inching along the top of the lever. Once he reached the rotten log, there was enough room for him to crawl to freedom.

Bruised, scraped and tired, he collapsed to the ground. As he looked up, the huge stone boulders appeared to be turning into jelly as they wobbled into a liquid blue-gray blur against the darkening sky. He felt like he was going to be sick.

"You'll be all right," comforted the little man, who was watching him curiously.

"I feel a little sick," responded Byron, shaking his head, "but I'm sure glad to be out of there. Thanks."

The little man helped Byron to his feet, then led him slowly along a little trail through the trees. Byron's legs were still pretty numb from lack of circulation.

They hadn't gone far when the wild man pushed aside some juniper branches and led Byron into a darkened cave. He struck a match and lit a candle that was standing in a little indentation in the stone wall. The cave wasn't very large, just over ten feet wide and about twenty feet long, the ceiling higher at the back than at the front.

"Make yourself comfortable," said the little man, motioning to a bed that was nothing more than a deerskin stretched across a mound of pine needles.

"My horse," said Byron, as he dropped to the bed. "I left him tied to a tree, still saddled, just up the draw from where I saw you standing on the rock."

"I'll take care of it," said the little man as he disappeared into the fading light of early evening. "There's a little meadow and a spring in the bottom of the draw. I'll tether him there...."

After making himself as comfortable as possible, Byron looked around the cave. In the middle was a stone fireplace with a chimney disappearing into the ceiling. Firewood was stacked from floor to ceiling all along one side of the cave. On the other side were some shelves where the man's belongings were kept.

On the top shelf Byron noticed a recurve bow and a deerskin quiver full of arrows. On the next shelf were plastic gallon jars full of dried chokecherries and jerky, and on the bottom shelf there were sacks of flour, sugar, salt and beans.

Near the fireplace stood a small plank table with a candle holder on each side and a stack of books at the back. Byron climbed painfully to his feet and hobbled over to the table. There was a Bible opened to the seventeenth chapter of Matthew. The volumes stacked at the back of the table were *The Complete Works of William Shakespeare, Paradise Lost* by John Milton, *Selected Writings of T.S. Eliot, Think and Grow Rich* by Napoleon Hill, and *Psycho-Cybernetics* by Maxwell Maltz.

Byron couldn't help but wonder why this wild man was living alone in a cave in the tops of the mountains. Maybe he was an outlaw, hiding from the law. Byron had heard of escaped convicts living in the wilds like this to avoid recapture. Perhaps the little man was a lunatic or an escapee from a mental institution.

It was dark outside when the little man returned. He lit more candles around the cave and stoked up the fire in the stone fireplace. He hung a black kettle over the flames, then seated himself on a wooden stool by the table.

"In a way," he said, "I'm glad you fell between those rocks. Haven't had a decent conversation with another human being in almost two years. What brings you up this way?"

"Was worrying about something," responded Byron, looking into the fire."Wanted some time by myself to sort things out."

Byron forced himself to sit up, reaching out to shake the hand of the strange little man.

"My name is Byron Horn," he said. The little man responded with a firm handshake.

"Chester Peabody is the name on the books at the courthouse," he responded."The forest rangers call me The Wasatch Savage. I'd appreciate you not telling them my real name or the whereabouts of this cave. They think I'm a trespasser and would like to catch me. I figure this land is as much mine as theirs. Besides, I'm not hurtin' anything."

He stood up and walked over to the bubbling pot. A delicious aroma was filling the cave. Using a wooden ladle, he filled two bowls.

"I'll keep your secret," promised Byron. "What's for supper?"

"Prime rib of porcupine goulash with rice and selected seasonings," replied the little man. "Specialty of the house." The Savage handed one of the steaming bowls to the reclining cowboy.

After finishing off a second steaming bowl of goulash, Byron leaned comfortably back against the cave wall and asked The Savage why he was living like a hermit in the tops of the mountains.

"I hope you don't think the law is after me, that I'm some kind of criminal," said The Savage.

"The thought has crossed my mind," responded Byron.

"I assure you that is not the case. But tell me what this big problem is that you think you have to come clear up here to sort it out."

Byron looked at The Savage. He liked this little man and felt like talking to him, realizing that it's often easier to talk to strangers than to those you are close to. With strangers things are simpler, without complications. You've never seen strangers before and probably will never see them again.

Byron told The Savage about his life's ambition to become a world champion bull rider, about his successful beginning and all the money he won the first two years in professional competition. Then he told about his unfortunate attempt to ride the white bull from Antelope Island, and about the serious injuries that resulted, about the weeks in the hospital, the intense pain--and now that he was well and ready to ride again, the pressure from friends and loved ones to give up bull riding. They wanted him to take up something more steady, marry his girlfriend and raise a family. Bull riding was too dangerous, unsteady and irregular in income, and it required constant travel--not a good profession for a man with a family.

"Do you love her?" asked The Savage.

"Who?" asked Byron after a pause.

"Your girlfriend--who else?"

"I suppose I do," said Byron, thoughtfully. "And I respect my parents."

Then there was resolution in his voice.

"But all my life, since I was a little kid, I've dreamed of becoming a world champion bull rider. I'm close to realizing that dream, maybe only a year or two away. And everybody wants me to give it up. Aren't there more important things in life than security and safety? I don't know what to do."

The Savage set a heavy log on the smoldering fire, removed the pot of porcupine stew, and set it aside to cool. There was enough left over for breakfast.

Looking thoughtfully into the fire, The Savage absent-mindedly plucked a few bristly hairs from his red beard.

"I can't tell you what to do," he said softly, not taking his eyes from the fire. "Decisions like that a man has to make for himself." He looked over at Byron.

"Sometimes you have to give up your dreams when something more important or pressing comes along. But sometimes you can give up your dreams too quickly, let people talk you out of something you really want. Then you're sorry later. That's what happened to me."

He walked back to the stool and sat down again. After looking blankly at the open Bible for a few moments, he looked over at Byron again, continuing, "My dream was to become a writer and inventor. A combination Mark Twain and Thomas Edison."

"You failed?"

The Savage hesitated before giving his answer.

"I don't think I failed. I just didn't stick with it

long enough.

"When I was a senior at the University of California, Berkeley," he continued,"everything seemed to be going my way. I was getting ready to graduate in physics and literature. I was dating the most beautiful girl on the tennis team. I was a well-known writer in one of the campus literary magazines and had started my first book. Even one of my inventions was making me over $3,000 a month, not bad for a student."

"What was it?" asked Byron.

The Savage grinned, the first time since Byron had met him. He stood up, facing Byron.

"Got an old A.B. Dick offset sheet press, one of the little ones, at a fire sale." He held his hands apart to indicate the size of the printing press."Remodeled it to take rolls of paper, like those in paper towel dispensers in rest rooms." The Savage was enthusiastic now.

"Welded on some knife blades and perforator bars so the paper would come off in three separate strips with perforations every four inches, like toilet paper. Then it would roll onto those cardboard inserts for toilet paper." The Savage looked at Byron, pausing to see if the young cowboy was catching the vision of what he was talking about.

"How did it make you $3,000 a month?" asked Byron, still not sure what The Savage had done with his remodeled printing press.

"That little machine produced custom-imprinted toilet paper, three rolls at a time. I put ads in the university newspaper, then some magazines. The orders started pouring in--three rolls for $12.95. The price included five words of typesetting and one photograph.

"Sold thousands and thousands of rolls with photos of Richard Nixon and the Ayatollah Khomeini printed on them. Employees would send me pictures of their bosses. Students would order rolls with their principal's face printed on each square. I'd even get orders from men who wanted me to print the faces of ex-girlfriends.

"But things really got busy at election time," The Savage continued. "Got lots of orders from political campaign committees with photos and copy on opponents they wanted smeared. Every time Jerry Brown ran for an office in California I got thousands of orders for rolls with his photo and the caption, "If it's Brown, flush it.""

Byron was laughing. The whole situation was so funny now. Not just the custom toilet paper, but the fact that the same guy who had been running a business like that was now living in a cave in the tops of the Utah mountains.

"Here, I'll show you another of my inventions," said The Savage as he skipped to the back of the cave and jerked a deerskin cover from a cot that Byron hadn't noticed earlier. After many months of being alone, The Savage was thoroughly enjoying the chance to talk to someone.

He brought the cot to the middle of the cave where Byron could get a good look at it. It was made of aluminum tubing with what appeared to be unnecessary hinges and cross pieces.

"Here's how it works," he said as he began folding it up. In a few seconds he had converted the cot into a pack rack, similar in appearance to the kind used by mountain climbers. He slipped the straps over his shoulders and started hiking around the cave.

"The backpacker carries his gear on it all day, then at night he folds it out into a comfortable cot, then back into a pack rack the next morning. It weighs only 1.2 pounds. It can be produced for less than $10, and could be sold for about $39 in most stores. Don't you think the sporting goods stores in this country could sell a million of these?"

"I'll bet they could," said Byron enthusiastically.

The Savage placed the cot back down on the ground
and covered it with the deerskin.

"What happened?" asked Byron. "Why are you
living in the mountains?"

"Well, like I said," began The Savage, his voice
more quiet now, "I had a lot going for me that last
year at Cal. I married the tennis player. She had looks,
personality, good grades, and was rich. She drove a
Mercedes to school. Her name was Mabel Monson.

"After graduation we were married and I went to
work finishing my book. Shipped the manuscript off
to a New York publisher, then went to work on this
cot. After two months the manuscript came back with
a standard rejection form clipped to the front page. I
could hardly believe my eyes. I had spent months
slaving over that manuscript and they didn't even
bother to tell me why they didn't want to publish it.
Well, I'd show them, I'd send it to another publisher,
and when it was making millions, that first publisher
would be awfully sorry and would beg for the opportunity to print my second book.

"While waiting to hear from the second publisher
I patented the pack rack. Had to sell Mabel's
Mercedes to pay the attorneys. The second publisher
rejected the book too, and so did the third, fourth and
fifth. In the meantime I couldn't get a manufacturer
interested in the pack rack.

"While I was having all these problems Mabel was
spending money just as freely as she had in school--
meals in fancy restaurants, weekend ski trips, fancy
new clothes for every occasion. We were going into
debt, fast. If it hadn't been for the money her father
sent her, I don't know what we would have done.

"Finally her father offered me a job in the family
business in Detroit. He had a company that built those
little knobs you pull up and down to lock and unlock
car doors. They made them out of plastic, steel, and
wood, in all shapes and colors, in every price range.

The knobs were sold to domestic and foreign car manufacturers, and Mr. Monson was very proud that his company controlled about 40 percent of the world door lock knob market.

"He said I could use his laboratory to develop my inventions, and that he might even help me produce and market some of them. I became excited about the job, accepted his offer. We packed our things and moved to Detroit."

Byron stretched out on his deerskin bed, listening with interest to The Savage's story. It had been a long time since The Savage had talked with anyone, and now that he had begun talking, the words flowed freely and easily. His story had been held inside long enough, and it felt good to finally tell it to someone.

"Mr. Monson started me out in quality control," he continued. "He said that would tie in with my physics background. I'm still not sure what checking colors and counting knobs has to do with physics, but it didn't seem to matter. I was taking home a fat paycheck every two weeks. I was paying off the debts and working on my inventions nights and weekends.

"Gradually I began to realize that the reason Mr. Monson gave me the job was to bring his daughter home, not because he needed or wanted my skills. I was given jobs to oversee things that didn't need overseeing. When I presented my inventions to the old man, he always wanted another marketing survey, or a more detailed cost analysis, or a new patent search. After two years it finally sank into my thick skull that he wasn't interested in my inventions. I began to realize that all he cared about was door lock knobs.

"In the meantime, Mabel and I began having problems. She was so busy with tennis tournaments, fashion shows and women's club functions that I seldom saw her, except when I made her sit down with me to discuss her spending habits. It didn't seem to matter how much her father paid me, she could always spend more. She was having a great time while I was experiencing a slow death.

"I thought that maybe having children would add more meaning to our lives and bring more happiness, but in her circle of friends, having children was an old-fashioned thing for dull people who didn't have anything better to do. She refused to have children."

The Savage was on his feet now, too engrossed in the telling of his story to stay still. He paced back and forth as he relived a critical period of his life. Byron continued to listen with interest.

"I began to escape my depressing situation by looking into the future and dreaming about the great things I was going to accomplish some day, the books I was going to write, the inventions that were going to change the world. Always 'someday.'

"But I never pinpointed when that 'someday' was going to be. I guess I was afraid, afraid that day would never come. Deep inside, I guess I was beginning to believe that I was nothing but a drone to a rich queen bee in a tennis dress, and would remain one for the remainder of my days.

"But I didn't let my mind entertain such hard, sobering thoughts very long. It was much more pleasant to dream about the great things I was going to accomplish 'someday.'

The Savage stopped and looked at Byron.

"I lived that way for ten years. The only happiness I had was the counterfeit joy of wandering dreams."

He began pacing again, hands behind his back, looking down in deep concentration.

"Then one night when Mabel was at a tennis club meeting, I started thumbing through my old school books. There was nothing good on television."

The Savage stopped beside the wooden table and picked up the book of T.S. Eliot poems.

"Ever read Eliot?" he asked.

"No," was Byron's quick reply. "Never went to college."

"Don't feel bad. Most college kids don't read him either, and when they do, usually for a class assignment, they don't care for his stuff. That's the way it was with me when I first read him.

"But you know, as I thumbed through his book that night in Detroit, something happened." He paused.

"What?" asked Byron, propping himself up on one elbow.

"I started reading a poem called 'The Love Song of J. Alfred Prufrock,' a poem that had put me to sleep when I was in school. But this time the words seemed to jump out from the page and sting me to the very core."

The Savage began to read,

"Time for you and time for me,
And time yet for a hundred indecisions,
And for a hundred visions and revisions,
Before the taking of toast and tea.
In the room the women come and go
Talking of Michelangelo.
And indeed there will be time
To wonder, "Do I dare?" and "Do I dare?"
Time to turn back and descend the stair,
With a bald spot in the middle of my hair."'

"Want to know why that poem grabbed me so?" asked The Savage.

Byron nodded.

"It was me. I'd never met T.S. Eliot, but J. Alfred Prufrock was me. I was almost embarrassed to read it, it described my situation so exactly. I couldn't have read that poem in front of a group of people any more than I could have danced naked in front of them. It was my secret self, the real self I had been hiding from myself and from others.''

He looked down at the book and began reading again.

'"Do I dare
Disturb the universe?
And I have known the eyes already, known them all--
The eyes that fix you in a formulated phrase,
And when I am formulated, sprawling on a pin,
When I am pinned and wriggling on the wall.
Then how should I begin
To spit out all the butt-ends of my days and ways?
I should have been a pair of ragged claws
Scuttling across the floors of silent seas.
Should I, after tea and cakes and ices,
Have the strength to force the moment to its crisis?
And I have seen the eternal Footman hold my coat,
  and snicker,
And in short, I was afraid...
No! I am not Prince Hamlet, nor was meant to be;
Am an attendant lord, one that will do
To swell a progress, start a scene or two,
Advise the prince; no doubt, an easy tool,
Deferential, glad to be of use,
Politic, cautious, and meticulous;
Full of high sentence, but a bit obtuse;
At times, indeed, almost ridiculous--
Almost at times the Fool.'"

The Savage began to read with more intensity.

'"I grow old...I grow old...
I shall wear the bottoms of my trousers rolled.
Shall I part my hair behind?
Do I dare to eat a peach?
I shall wear white flannel trousers,
and walk upon the beach.'"

The Savage slammed the book down on the table.

"As I read that poem I knew it was me, every word of it. Not only was my life nothing, but I wasn't even enjoying it. I became angry. I was furious at myself for what I had become, or perhaps more accurately, for what I had not become.

"I decided it was time for a change, time to 'disturb the universe,' time to 'force the moment to its crisis.'

"I laid awake all night trying to figure out what I needed to do. It was one thing to feel bold after reading a poem, but quite another to actually do something about it. What should I say to Mr. Monson? What should I say to Mabel? Then the thought occurred me, why should I have to say or explain anything to anybody? That's when I decided what I must do. By the time the plan was formulated in every detail, it was time to get up."

Chapter 9

Byron was sitting up now, totally engrossed in The Savage's story. The Savage was pacing vigorously, casting darting shadows back and forth across the cave walls. Only two candles remained burning.

"While Mabel was still asleep," he continued, "I packed my favorite books and some personal belongings into my briefcase, then went into the garage and threw my pack rack into the trunk of my car. I then returned to the house and got ready for work as usual.

"I remember wondering as I kissed Mabel goodbye if I would ever see her again, and not really caring. She pushed me away, telling me to hurry so I wouldn't be late for work. I left without another word.

"I stopped at the corner and called the factory from a pay phone, telling them I wouldn't be in for awhile because I had some errands to take care of downtown.

"An hour later I was at the bank borrowing four thousand dollars, using the title to my car as security. With the money in my briefcase, I returned to the car, retrieved the pack rack from the trunk, tossed the keys down a storm sewer, and took a taxi to the airport.

"Using the name of A. Prufrock, I bought a one-way ticket to Salt Lake City."

"Why Salt Lake?" asked Byron.

"Lots of beautiful mountains. Saw a ski film once with hundreds of miles of beautiful mountains. Not very many people, except for the narrow strip west of the mountains. An easy place to get lost. And no reason for Mabel and her father to look for me there.

"From the airport, I caught a bus south to Provo, outfitted myself at the local stores, then headed into the mountains. Forest rangers ran me out of a couple of places, but they haven't found this cave yet."

"But why do you want to live out here in the wilds?" asked Byron. "Why didn't you just go to some little town and start where you left off before you married Mabel, get your printing press going again? That customized toilet paper sounds like a pretty good business."

"It made a lot of money, all right," said The Savage thoughtfully. "And I guess if all I cared about was making money, I could have gone back to it." He looked at Byron, his eyes fierce.

"But I figured there had to be more to life than making money. Besides, the customized toilet paper business fed on people's hate for each other. It wasn't a clean business, if you know what I mean."

"Like door lock knobs?" asked Byron, not meaning to sound sarcastic, but that's the way it came out, regardless.

"Door lock knobs are too clean," responded The Savage without hesitation. "No substance, no meaning, no excitement. The thought of spending a lifetime making and selling door lock knobs is enough to drive a man out of his mind, as almost happened to me."

"Don't you get lonely, living all by yourself like this?" asked Byron, changing the subject.

"The first year was bad. Just about packed up and headed back more than once. But I think I'm getting used to it. Still, it has been good to talk to you. Didn't realize how much I missed having someone to talk to."

"I've enjoyed listening to you," said Byron sincerely.

"That reminds me," he continued. "What was all that shouting business when I found you on that big rock this afternoon?"

"Oh that," said The Savage, looking down, picking his words carefully. "A long story. Do you really want to know?"

Byron nodded.

"You won't laugh at me?"

"Do you really care if I do?"

"Yes."

"I won't."

"When I came here," The Savage began, "I was determined to get to the bottom of things, to find some real meaning in life, get ahold of something I could get my teeth into. To push matters to a conclusion, to find out once and for all what life is all about.

"I read a lot of books but kept coming back to the Bible, mostly the New Testament and the words of Jesus. There's a man who knew what he was up to. Most of my time now is spent wrestling out an understanding of the things he taught so subtly, building enough faith to do the things he did."

"From custom toilet paper to religious fanaticism," exclaimed Byron.

"You promised not to laugh at me."

"I'm not laughing," explained Byron. "I'm just amazed at the wide range of your experience and focus."

"See where that Bible is opened to," said The Savage, pointing to his scriptures.

"Matthew 17," said Byron, still remembering the place.

"A man brought his son to the disciples to be healed," explained The Savage. "They couldn't do it, so the man took the boy to Jesus, who cured him instantly. After the man was gone, the disciples asked Jesus why they had been unable to heal the boy."

The Savage paused in his story for a moment, then looking directly at Byron, asked, "Do you believe Jesus really did the things the Bible says he did?"

"Sure," said Byron. "I've never read it all, but I

studied it in seminary, like most of the Mormon kids in Spanish Fork. I'm a believer."

"Then listen to this," said The Savage, open Bible in hand, turning to face Byron, "'And Jesus said unto them, because of your unbelief: for verily I say unto you, If ye have faith as a grain of mustard seed, ye shall say unto this mountain, Remove hence to yonder place; and it shall remove; and nothing shall be impossible unto you. Howbeit this kind goeth not out but by prayer and fasting.'"

The Savage closed the Bible and sat down on his stool.

"As I said earlier, I've been trying to build faith, the real stuff. This morning as I walked out of the cave I was at the end of a three-day period of fasting and praying. I really felt like I finally had as much faith as a grain of mustard seed. When I went up on the hill, I felt like I had enough faith to move that mountain."

"Hey, wait a minute," interrupted Byron. "Do you mean you were trying to command that mountain across the valley to move when I found you today?"

"That's right," said The Savage unashamedly.

"You're crazy," said Byron, starting to get up from his bed, until the stiffness in his legs reminded him that he should stay down.

"Would you like to read it for yourself?" said The Savage, offering the Bible to Byron. "Do you think I'm reading it wrong? Don't you think Jesus said that?"

"Sure he said it," said Byron, a note of hesitation in his voice. "But he probably meant something symbolic. He was probably talking about the symbolic mountains in each of our lives."

"Possibly," said The Savage carefully. "But there are also real mountains. Jesus said that those who followed him would do greater things than he did. He walked on water, raised the dead, turned water into wine, and much more. He could have moved real mountains too. When he said we could move mountains, I think that's exactly what he meant, and I aim to develop the faith to do it."

"Don't you think you could do a better job of it living in society, learning from religious leaders, engaging in Christian service?" asked Byron.

"There is a time for that kind of life, but not for me now," said The Savage with confidence, evidence he had asked himself that question many times before.

"There comes a time in every man or woman's life," he continued boldly, "when he or she must stop listening to others and seek out God. Moses was in the wilderness for forty years before returning to Egypt to free the children of Israel. Elijah and Jeremiah spent much time in the wilds. So did John the Baptist. Even Jesus fasted in the wilderness for forty days and nights before beginning his ministry."

"And you think you need to do it too," said Byron. "Many times I have the feeling that I'm preparing for some kind of ministry too, but I don't know what it is yet. I don't have enough faith, not even as much as a grain of mustard seed. But someday I will. Then watch out--you'll be hearing from me."

"You look tired," said The Savage, standing up. "Let's get some sleep." He blew out the candles.

The next morning, after finishing off the porcupine goulash, the two men hiked down to the meadow where the horse had been grazing. Byron's legs were still a little stiff from his accident, but otherwise he felt great.

It was a brilliant cloudless day, the sheer cliffs glowing in the morning sun. The little stream in the bottom of the canyon sparkled like a river of diamonds. Byron enjoyed the company of his new friend. Religious fanatic or not, he liked The Savage.

When the horse was saddled, the two men shook hands.

"Have you decided what you're going to do about your bull riding?" asked The Savage.

"Yes, I think I have," responded Byron, kicking thoughtfully at the sod. "As you said last night, sometimes a man has to give up his personal dreams and make way for more important matters. But I suppose that that time, at least for me, has not yet arrived." He looked into The Savage's face. "If I gave my dreams up now, I might end up feeling like you did in Detroit."

Byron put his foot in the stirrup and swung into the saddle. Holding the eager horse back and looking into the eyes of the red-bearded Savage, he said, "Next time you see this horse coming down the trail, he'll be carrying a world champion bull rider."

Byron loosened the reins and the horse lunged forward up the little trail.

"And next time you ride into this canyon," shouted The Savage after the departing rider, "Don't be surprised if one of the mountains is missing."

Chapter 10

It was late October, 1982, normally the quiet time of the year at Spanish Fork Fairgrounds. Dozens of cars and pickups were parked in the graveled area north of the arena. Vehicles had been coming in and out all day, bringing people who wanted to get a look at Moby Dick, the world-famous bucking bull, the same one Bill Thunder had called Medicine Bull.

It was in this arena, less than a year earlier, that many of these same spectators had witnessed the bull's introduction to rodeo. No one had ridden him then, nor had anyone ridden him since, though dozens of attempts had been made at the biggest rodeos in the United States and Canada.

Of the five cowboys who tried to ride Moby Dick at the Calgary Stampede, the average riding time was 3.8 seconds, less then half of the required eight seconds. At the Days of '47 Rodeo in Salt Lake City, two cowboys were dumped before the bull was all the way out of the gate. Every cowboy who tried to ride him in Cheyenne was hospitalized. During the bull's week at Madison Square Garden, three of the five cowboys who drew him refused to ride. At the Cow Palace in San Francisco he injured two of the nation's top rodeo clowns. He had even upended several mounted hazers as he become increasingly difficult to get back into the bucking chutes.

His exploits won him national fame, and during the season Moby Dick received more publicity than Boy George and Howard Cosell combined. His picture was on the cover of Time Magazine. There was a feature article about him in Reader's Digest, and another on the front page of the Wall Street Journal, as well as numerous articles and photos on the AP and UPI news wires.

By early July, the bull's presence at a rodeo guaranteed a sell-out crowd. The people cheered him more than they did the poor cowboys who tried bravely to ride him.

Moby Dick was owned by Morton Wilder of southern Utah County. Morton had bought the bull directly from the meat packer after watching Byron Horn's attempted ride early that year. Morton had paid $1200 for Moby Dick, who was now worth more than any bucking bull alive. Morton had recently turned down an offer of $190,000 for the bull.

Morton Wilder had been a small-time rodeo producer up until the purchase of Moby Dick. As the bull's fame spread, Morton was booked by more and more of the big rodeos. With the increased revenues, he aggressively replaced the weak buckers in his string with the best bulls money could buy. Now, after just one season, his bulls were considered by many to be the best in the business.

Moby Dick was being penned at the fairgrounds for several days to let the home fans have a look at their world-famous bucking bull before the national rodeo finals in Oklahoma City. Morton had brought his animals home for a few weeks of rest and recuperation before the world championships.

Another reason for the trip back to Utah was to allow a camera crew from Los Angeles to shoot some film of Moby Dick for a popular weekly television show called "The A Team."

Byron drove alone to the fairgrounds in his 1973 Dodge Power Wagon pickup. He turned in at the south end of the auction barns and parked just south of the holding corrals where the bucking stock was kept during rodeo events.

After hopping the outer fence, Byron walked directly to the bucking pens behind the announcer's stand. He wanted to see Moby Dick too. To Byron, the bull was more than a national celebrity coming home. It was an opponent that had beaten him badly, nearly killed him. And now that Byron had decided to get back in the race for the national bull riding title the coming spring, he figured there was a pretty good chance he would have the opportunity to ride this bull again.

It didn't take Byron long to locate the corral with the solitary white bull. Moby Dick had private quarters now, not just because he was worth a lot of money, but mainly because of the numerous injuries he inflicted on other bulls when battles broke out. His battle training among the bison had cost Morton Wilder a lot of money in vet bills.

Byron climbed to the top of the fence and looked down upon the great Moby Dick, who was busy chewing on alfalfa hay. Byron had half-expected the $190,000 bull to look the part of a manicured show bull. On the contrary, his battle-scarred hide was filthy with dirt and manure. It wasn't that Morton didn't want to clean up his world-famous bull for its own homecoming party. He just wasn't able to find a groom foolish enough to lay a comb and brush to the dusty hide.

Several groups of people were standing just outside the fence, watching the famous bull between the boards. As Byron observed the 2,000-pound beast munching quietly on the hay, he imagined himself climbing down on the broad, muscled back. His thigh muscles tightened. His left hand curled into a tight fist as if he were grasping his rigging. He felt a tinge of adrenalin surge through his body. He was relaxed, alert and intent, ready to take on any opponent, including the white bull that had almost ruined his bull riding career.

Byron was glad he didn't have to ride the bull on this particular afternoon. He wasn't ready yet. But he knew he would be ready when the time came.

"Someday," Byron said just loud enough for the

bull to hear him, but not the other people. "Someday, I'll draw you for a ride. My spurs'll be so deep in your shoulders you'll never shake me loose. Never. That's a promise." The bull continued to munch on the hay, paying no heed to the determined young man.

Byron jumped to the ground and strode quickly back to his pickup. The time of soul-searching, pondering and self-introspection had come to an end. He had a lot of work to do if he was going to be a serious contender for the world championship bull riding crown.

Chapter 11

There were several alternatives open to Byron in preparing himself for world championship bull riding. There were professional bull riding schools, each class usually lasting several weeks, during which the students rode several bulls every day with their performance videotaped. The rest of the time was spent in the classroom going over the videotapes with an instructor.

There were several of the better schools Byron would have liked to attend, but a summer of being injured and unable to work had left him broke. He had no choice but to tune up his riding skills the old way.

After leaving the fairgrounds where Moby Dick was still feeding on alfalfa, Byron picked up his little brother, Billy, then drove to their uncle's farm near the mouth of Spanish Fork Canyon. After saddling two horses, they galloped out into the 200-acre pasture behind the house and gathered six bulls out of the grazing herd of cattle, chasing them into the corrals behind the barn, where there was a bucking chute. Among the six bulls there Herefords, shorthorns and one big Holstein. With Billy working the gate and the stopwatch, Byron started riding bulls for the first time since his injury.

It was late afternoon when Byron mounted the sixth bull. He had ridden four of the first five for the required eight seconds, and now as he climbed upon the sixth, a 1700-pound shorthorn, his confidence was strong but his arm and legs were tired.

As soon as he had a firm grip on the rigging he nodded for Billy to open the gate. Byron's form was good for the first four jumps, then the angry shorthorn ducked into a sudden counter-clockwise spin. Byron couldn't hang on and sommersaulted into the dust. Instinctively, Byron looked back towards the bull. It was trotting towards him, head high, ears forward. Byron scooped up a handful of dirt, which he threw into the beast's face as soon as it was in range. The bull turned away.

Byron knew from previous experience with this animal that it was a bluffer. The big Holstein was not. One of the hardest things about going on the road and riding strange bulls was never knowing for sure if the bull beneath you would go for blood or if he was just a bluffer. Billy opened the gate to let the shorthorn out in the pasture with the other cattle.

Bull riding became a daily routine for Byron. With Billy coming down after school to work the gate, Byron rode an average of five bulls every day. Some of them became tired of bucking after a while and had to be replaced with wilder bulls. Some would buck hard every day, while others only had enough ambition to buck hard once every two or three days. There were more bulls in the pasture, though, so for a while Byron didn't have any trouble finding the ones that would buck with him.

In late November as the weather got colder and the days shorter, Byron began looking for an inside arena to practice in. Soon the ground would be frozen and as hard as a concrete slab.

It didn't take Byron long to locate an arena near Payson, on the Hays Hereford Ranch. The Hays brothers told Byron he could use the arena as much as he wished as long as he was through by 6 p.m. on Tuesdays and Thursdays, when the barn was used for steer team roping.

They also gave Byron use of one of the corrals near

the bucking chute to keep the bulls in. After bringing in five of the best buckers from the herd at his uncle's ranch, Byron started rounding up some big exotic-bred bulls from local ranches. The standard arrangement was that Byron would feed the bulls in exchange for being permitted to ride them.

It seemed that only the ranchers who knew Byron and wanted to help him agreed to such terms. Even though they would save hay by not having to feed the bulls, there were two good reasons for not letting Byron take a bull. First, there was a high rate of injury among bucking bulls. Few ranchers were willing to risk serious injury to their bulls merely to save a little hay. Second, bucking bulls were inclined to become mean when handled roughly by chute men and riders. No rancher in his right mind wanted his bulls to become meaner.

Nevertheless, Byron's persistence paid off and he soon had another eight bulls in the corral with his uncle's range bulls. His goal was to attempt to ride five of the thirteen bulls every day. Byron already felt that he was riding as well as he had before his injury, but he also knew he would have to get a lot better if he hoped to become a world champion bull rider, especially if he hoped to ride the great Moby Dick.

Billy soon tired of helping with the gate everyday, and that wasn't a job Byron could give to just anyone. If the gate was opened too quickly, the bull might not get turned around enough and might sideswipe the gate post during the first buck, greatly increasing the chances of injury to the cowboy and the bull. If the gate was opened too slowly, the bull might break a horn or even fall down in his mad scramble to get turned around in too small an opening.

A few of the cowboys that Byron would see from time to time knew how to open bucking gates, but since none of them could be counted on for steady gate-opening chores day after day, Byron rigged up a system of ropes, springs and pulleys that enabled him to open the gate by himself by tugging on a rope over the chute when he was ready to come out.

Byron arrived at the barn about 2 p.m. every afternoon. After hazing the bulls he intended to ride into a holding pen behind the bucking chute, he broke open several bales of alfalfa hay in the pen he had just driven them from. As soon as he finished riding a bull, he let it return to the pen with the hay. This was the only time Byron fed the bulls, so they were always very hungry as they entered the bucking chute and therefore very eager to return to their corral and the hay as soon as Byron was no longer on their backs.

Thus Byron eliminated the problem of wasting a lot of time chasing bulls out of the arena to clear the way for his next ride. All he had to do was open the gate leading to the delicious hay and the bull gladly trotted to the chow without any coaxing. It took about three times for a new bull to learn this routine.

After the hay was down and the first bull was in the chute, Byron was ready to begin his daily rides. If there were no other people around, he would usually delay the first ride for a while, hoping that someone might come. He always felt better coming out of the chute if he knew someone else was around. Not that he needed anyone for any of the routine matters, but if he were to become injured, it would be handy to have someone around to chase off an angry bull, administer first aid, or call an ambulance or doctor.

If no one was around by the end of a half hour or so, Byron would begin riding anyway. Since he didn't have a buzzer to tell him when his eight seconds were up, he just tried to ride a good ten or twelve seconds before bailing out, being careful to dodge the occasional departing kick that sometimes came his way before the bull trotted off to eat its evening meal.

Byron's strategy to become a world champion bull rider was well-planned. He believed it was dedicated and disciplined athletes, not rough and tough cowboys fresh off the range, who won world championships.

Byron knew that other bull riders practiced to some degree during the off season. Some went to bull riding schools or ran their own schools. Some had training programs similar to Byron's wherein they attempted to ride a certain number of bulls every day.

As Byron got to know some of the best riders during his first years in professional rodeo, he learned that they all had one thing in common, even the champions who participated in the world championships in Oklahoma City. Without exception, Byron had never heard of any of these training programs that lasted very long. A bull rider might go to a school for a few weeks, riding two or three bulls a day. Then he would lay off for a while. Then he might set up a program in a rancher's back pasture similar to Byron's program of riding a given number of bulls every day. Without exception, Byron had never heard of any of these training programs lasting more than a month. There were just too many problems that plagued such training plans. Bulls became tired of bucking and had to be replaced. Plus, any cowboy who tries to ride bulls every day for a month is almost certain to receive injuries: cracked ribs, wrenched knees, sprained wrists, torn ligaments, and all the other injuries experienced in contact sports, plus the more serious step-on injuries: ruptured spleens, fractured breastbones, and so on. When a bull rider is nursing one or more of these types of injuries, it's difficult to sustain a daily training program.

Byron's plan was to maintain a five-bull-a-day riding program over a five-month period. As far as he knew, no one had ever even come close to riding that many bulls during a single off season. He knew that if he could maintain such a schedule without injury he would enter the coming professional bull riding season better prepared and in better condition than probably any bull rider in the history of bull riding. He knew the key to maintaining such a program was keeping injuries to a minimum.

Luck was with Byron through the remainder of November and all of December. His most severe injury was a cracked rib.

His training program began every morning with a mile run in his snow boots. When the temperature was below 20 degrees, he wore a face mask to protect his lungs fom the icy air. When the temperature dropped below zero on two occasions he skipped rope in the garage for ten minutes.

After breakfast Byron helped his uncle with feeding and other chores until noon. In exchange, his uncle paid him $50 a week, provided hay for the bulls, and let Byron use his stock truck for hauling the animals.

Byron gave up sweets, late hours, dating and partying. He was an athlete in training. His muscle tone was perfect. His mind was clear and alert. All his senses were sharpened. His food tasted better. The air smelled cleaner. The sky looked bluer. He didn't get sleepy during the day, but at night he slept soundly and deeply.

Byron's superb physical conditioning gave him a sense of well-being and vitality unknown to those who deaden their bodies with lack of exercise and too much alcohol, caffeine, junk food and worry.

The biggest problem with his training was keeping a string of bulls that wanted to buck. Few bulls would buck hard everyday, even when the rider used his spurs. Most would do their best only if ridden several times a week, and some not even that frequently. But all the bulls got used to Byron after a while.

They eventually learned that no matter how hard they bucked, Byron would jump off after eight or ten seconds, anyway. The rare bull that could throw Byron once in a while tended to buck harder in the hope of getting rid of the rider early. The rest, however, were inclined to give up, like horses being broke to ride. When this happened, these bulls were returned to their owners and replaced with fresh ones. In jest, local ranchers would frequently ask each other that winter if they had any bulls needing to be broke to ride. If so, Byron Horn would do it for nothing, along with feeding the bull too.

By mid-January fresh bulls were getting harder and harder to find. Byron had only seven bulls that bucked with any spirit, and several of those were rapidly losing ambition.

Early one afternoon, as Byron was driving along the highway south of Spanish Fork, he started thinking about Morton Wilder, the rodeo producer who owned Moby Dick. Byron had never met the man. Morton owned a lot of bucking bulls and Byron thought that since good hay was up to $80 a ton, perhaps Mr. Wilder would be willing to let Byron borrow several of his bucking bulls in exchange for feeding them. In addition, the bulls would get some good bucking practice to get them in shape for the coming season.

As Byron turned off the highway onto the country road leading to the Wilder ranch, he remembered some of his cowboy friends talking about Morton Wilder's beautiful daughter. If he remembered correctly, her name was Karen. But his thoughts didn't dwell on the daughter very long. He had more important matters to think about.

Chapter 12

As Byron drove under the huge cedar log archway, the entrance to the Wilder ranch, he couldn't help but notice many signs of recently acquired wealth: new pickups and cars, freshly painted house and barns, new six-pole corrals.

Byron felt uneasy as he walked across the wooden porch and knocked on the oak door. He wasn't sure why, but he sensed that Morton Wilder was not going to be enthusiastic about loaning his bucking bulls. But it was too late to turn back. He rang the doorbell.

It wasn't Morton Wilder who answered the door, but his daughter Karen. She was a sophomore at Utah State University, but had dropped out for the winter quarter to help her father line up his summer and fall rodeo bookings.

Karen was wearing faded blue jeans, western boots, a clean white blouse, and a blue and white checkered scarf wrapped over the top of her head and tied behind, holding her long black hair in place.

"Hi," said Byron as he looked into her clear hazel eyes. He was only a few years older than the girl, but he had never met her before.

He couldn't help but notice her smooth complexion and firm mouth. She was not thin, nor was there any unnecessary bulk to her womanly figure. She had a pleasant smile. Byron liked what he saw.

Byron was so engrossed in digesting his first impression of Karen Wilder that he was unaware of the passage of time. That wasn't like Byron. An awkward silence developed. Finally Karen broke the spell.

"Is there anything I can do for you?" she asked, just a touch of mockery in her voice. She was enjoying the intensity of his attention.

Her words fell on Byron like cinder blocks as he suddenly became aware of the awkward pause he had created. His face turned crimson, first from embarrassment, then from his anger at having blushed. He felt foolish.

"My name is Byron Horn," he finally blurted out. "I would like to talk to Mr. Wilder."

"Come in," said Karen as she stepped back into the house. "Father's on the phone, but he should be through in a few minutes."

She led the young cowboy to a sofa in a big hallway and motioned for him to sit down. He did so, removing his hat and unzipping his parka. She didn't offer to take his coat.

Byron could hear a man's voice coming from a room at the end of the hall; apparently Morton Wilder was talking on the phone. Again Byron felt an awkward silence developing, and as before, the moment was saved by Karen, who sensed his uneasiness.

"I'm Karen," she said politely. "Aren't you the cowboy who's been riding five bulls a day over at the Hays ranch?"

"That's me," said Byron, smiling, flattered that she knew about his training program. "But it's getting more difficult. I'm running out of bulls willing to buck for me."

"Even three a day is a lot," said Karen. "How in the world can you ride that many bulls day after day without getting hurt?"

"It's not as hard as you might think," said Byron. "My bulls aren't very tough. They're just ordinary range bulls with a little buck in them. They're not high-powered rodeo bulls like those your father owns."

Byron wondered why he minimized the danger of

what he was doing when he felt such an urge to im-
press this girl.

"How's Moby Dick?" he asked.

"He's looking good," she said. "A little fat
perhaps, but stronger than ever. He should have a
good season again."

"Do you think anyone will ride him this year?"

"Dad doesn't think anyone will ever ride him, but
I imagine someday he'll get tired of bucking and let a
cowboy stay on him for eight seconds. Still, I doubt it
will be this year." She paused for a moment, then
said, "Follow me. Dad's off the phone now."

When Byron entered the office, Morton Wilder
was leaning back in a swivel chair, his feet propped
comfortably on top of a mahogany desk. He was a
husky middle-aged man with a normal paunch from
lack of physical activity. His hair was black and bushy
but neatly cropped. There was lots of color in his
weather-worn cheeks and plenty of spark in his hazel
eyes. Wilder withdrew his feet from the desk and
stood to greet Byron.

After shaking hands with the young bull rider,
Wilder dropped back into his chair and eased his boots
back onto the desk. "What can I do for you?" he asked
as Byron took a chair across from the desk. The girl remained standing by the door.

"You may have heard about my training program
at the Hays ranch," began Byron,"how I feed and
board bulls in exchange for being able to ride them.
I'm trying to ride five bulls a day. I've been doing that
until just recently. Hard to keep enough bulls that will
buck...."

"Wait a minute," interrupted Wilder. "If you've
come here to ask me to lend you some of my bucking
bulls to practice on, you're barking up the wrong tree.
Even if I was short of hay I wouldn't be interested."

"Thank you for your time," said Byron coldly, getting up to leave.

"Not so fast," said Wilder, motioning for Byron to sit back down. "Stay a minute and I'll tell you a few things about bull riding."

Byron didn't want to sit down again, but he didn't want to be rude in front of the girl, either, so he sat back down. He pretended to be picking at a piece of lint on his knee as he waited for Wilder to speak.

"I've got plenty of hay this year," began Wilder, "but even if I didn't I wouldn't let you take any of my bulls.

"If I loaned you my bulls," he continued, "two things would happen. The bulls would become more gentle in their bucking, and you would become a better rider. Gentle bulls and skilled riders are the two most dangerous threats to my business."

He paused for a moment as he fished for a big cigar in the top drawer of his desk. Without lighting it, he shoved it in his mouth and began to chew thoughtfully. "You see," he said, "my income is directly proportional to the number of paying customers my animals draw into the rodeo grandstands. Contrary to what you cowboys think, the majority of paying fans don't flock to rodeo arenas to watch cowboys ride bulls." He paused, continuing to look directly at Byron.

"What they really want to see," he continued, "is the riders getting thrown off, trampled, gored, kicked and chased. They want to see mean bulls throwing cowboys in every direction. That's when they stand up yelling, stomping and spilling their drinks.

"Believe me, Byron, I know what I'm talking about. When I can put together a rank string of bulls for the first night of a three-day rodeo, a bunch so rank and mean that not a single rider can hang on for eight seconds that first night, the next two nights are guaranteed sellouts. It happens every time, without fail.

"If you take my good bulls over to your arena and by riding them everyday take some of the rankness out of them, it's going to be harder for me to put that winning string together. If I don't fill the stands, then it's going to be tough to get back into that rodeo the next year.

"Why do you think Moby Dick is worth so much?" he continued. "You probably read in the papers where I was offered $190,000 for him. That comes out to $95 a pound. That's expensive beefsteak, by anybody's standards." Wilder paused a moment for his words to sink in.

"I turned down that $95 a pound offer because that white devil is going to make me a lot more than that this year alone and who knows how much next year, or the year after."

Byron listened with interest as Morton Wilder continued to talk about his bull.

"That bull is the biggest rodeo attraction since Annie Oakley. And that's not because he's a nice feller who lets people ride him. It's because nobody can ride him. And he bucks them off with style. He butts, gores, tramples and kicks. That's what people pay to see, more than anything else."

"That's the way you see it," said Byron.

"It's a good thing for me there are not more riders like you," said Wilder, conviction in his voice. "Kids who work their hearts out to become champions. If bull riders as a whole got good enough where they could ride bulls like mine eighty percent of the time, bull riding would probably cease to be the most popular rodeo sport. It would become a ho-hum part of the program, like barrel racing and steer roping, like watching the band at a football game half-time."

Byron stood up. "I'm sorry to disappoint you," he said. "You may earn your bread with bulls that no one can ride, but I earn mine by riding bulls, whether they be yours or someone else's." Byron turned to leave.

"Sit down," ordered Wilder, a friendly manner in his voice. "I'm not going to give you any of my bulls, but I've got a proposition you might be interested in."

Byron sat down for the third time. During Wilder's lecture, Karen had left the room. The two men were alone now. Byron felt more at ease with the girl gone. In fact, he was beginning to enjoy Wilder's blunt, easy manner.

Deep in thought, Wilder was staring blankly into space, his jaws working without pause on the soggy, unlit cigar. Byron waited patiently for the older man to speak.

"As time goes on," began Wilder thoughtfully, "there are going to be more and more kids like you who take bull riding serious enough to learn how to do it right. The days of the cowhand going down to the local fairgrounds to ride a few bulls for a little prize money are gone. The big purses are going to professional athletes, some of whom don't even know how to saddle a horse. It's amazing the improvement that bull riders as a whole have undergone the last few years. And as more and more go into serious off-season training, as you have done, the better they are going to get.

"On the other side of the coin," continued Wilder, thinking out loud, "the bulls are not getting any better. Sure, there is a Moby Dick once in a while that no one can ride, but on the whole bulls are about the same today as they were ten years ago, except in size, thanks to the growing popularity of the larger exotic breeds of cattle.

"But one of these days, as the riders get better and the bulls stay the same, bull riding is going to lose much of its appeal."

"You're breaking my heart," said Byron. "I hope you're not trying to talk me out of my training program."

"Not at all," said Wilder easily and Byron sensed

the producer was still holding back the main point of the conversation.

"Byron, have you ever read about those fighting bulls they raise in Spain?"

"A little," responded Byron.

"Those black devils are so agile, vicious and mean they're allowed to fight only once, on the day they're killed. They learn so much during that first fight in the ring that if they were allowed to live and fight again, they would become so deadly that even the best of matadors would refuse to fight them. They handle their horns with the dexterity of an experienced swordfighter, and as soon as they can figure out what's going on in the arena, experienced bull fighters start backing away. The agility, speed and cunning of these bulls is incomprehensible to those of us who have only had experience with breeds of cattle developed over centuries for docility, meat and milk production. There is no comparison between our domestic bulls and those Spanish bulls that have been bred for nothing but fighting. If someone would take one of those Spanish bulls and use it for bull riding, I think you would find that after about the third time out of the chute, it would be killing riders, pinning clowns to the fence, and disemboweling pick-up horses."

Byron said nothing, wondering why Wilder was telling him all this.

"To come to the point, Byron," said Wilder. "I'm trying to tell you that I believe that through selective breeding a superior bucking bull can be produced that will keep bull riding the number one rodeo attraction and keep you cowboys spitting dirt for many generations. Do you agree with me?"

"You've got the right sire to start such a breed," said Byron without hesitation. "As far as I know there's never been a bucking bull as good as this Moby Dick."

also got to have the right kind of cow to breed him to, and that's my problem.''

"What are you getting at?'' asked Byron.

"I've got 87 cows in the pasture out there,'' said Wilder, pointing to the window. "Most of them are exotics with good size, but I don't want any of them in my breeding program with Moby Dick until they have proven their dispositions and athletic ability to be characteristic of good bucking stock. I've got to find out which cows are most likely to produce good buckers. For a selective breeding program you've got to be able so select the ones you want from the ones you don't want.''

"How are you going to do that?'' asked Byron.

"That's where you come in....''

"Oh no you don't,'' interrupted Byron. "I ride bulls, not cows.''

"Don't knock my cows,'' said Wilder. "They're young, they're big, they're fleshy. There are several of them pushing 1500 pounds. That's a lot of cow, and even though I don't know for sure, I'd be willing to bet that some of them will buck as good as some of the better bucking bulls. They have the agility and size to do it. They're young and strong. Besides, maybe it's time we give women's liberation a chance by giving the cows a chance to show us what they can do.'' Wilder laughed at his own attempt at humor.

"What do you want me to do?'' asked Byron, beginning to show a little interest but not much.

"You need animals to ride and I need someone to evaluate the bucking ability of my cows,'' said Wilder. "Let's get together. Tomorrow I'll truck eight or ten cows out to the Hays ranch and you work them into your bucking program as you would bulls. Weed out the ones that don't perform, keep the good buckers as long as you need them. Once a week I'll send a truck out to pick up the culls and drop off some fresh ones for you to try out. What do you think?''

"Interesting," said Byron, shrugging his shoulders in non-commitment.

"I'll provide you with plenty of animals to practice on, and you'll be helping me select my breeding stock."

"I don't know," responded Byron thoughtfully. "I just don't know if those cows can buck hard enough to give me the kind of practice I need."

"I'll pay you a dollar a day for each cow you've got," offered Wilder. "That ought to cover your hay bill. Try it for a few weeks. We may find out that some of these cows have more buck in them than a lot of bulls. I'll send Karen out with a load of cows tomorrow. What do you say?"

Morton Wilder reached out to shake hands with Byron.

"A deal?"

Byron still had his doubts about the cows being able to buck hard enough to help him in his training, but when Wilder said Karen would be bringing out the cows, Byron suddenly felt good about giving the proposal a try. Byron took Wilder's hand. "We'll try it for a week or two and see what happens," he said.

As Byron walked to the door, he hoped he would see Karen again, but she was nowhere in sight.

Chapter 13

After throwing a bale of hay into the bull pen at the Hays barn, Byron climbed onto the fence to watch the bulls eat. Normally they didn't get any hay until after Byron had ridden them, but today the bulls were getting the day off. Karen Wilder was bringing a load of big young cows for Byron to ride.

It was early February and Byron had been riding five or six bulls a day for over two months. Most of them were easy to ride, but even the tough ones seldom threw Byron. He was in perfect physical condition, his muscles hard as steel. His body responded instinctively to every move the bulls made as they tried to dump him. His intensive riding program was paying off. Byron could hardly wait for the rodeo season to begin. He was a better rider than he had ever been before, even before his injury. He knew he would be one of the top money winners, and figured his time had finally come to qualify for the world championships in Oklahoma City the coming fall.

Byron didn't figure Morton Wilder's cows would buck hard enough to really test his riding skills, but fresh bulls were scarce. The cows would take the pressure off of having to find new bulls. And the dollar a day he received for keeping each cow would help out a lot.

Everything seemed to be working well, except for one thing. Karen Wilder. He was disturbed with the unsettling effect she had on him.

He had sworn off girls as part of his training program. He had neither the time, the money, nor the emotional energy to spend on women. He was devoting everything he had to becoming a world champion bull rider.

Byron figured many of the good bull riders never made it big because of their girlfriends or wives. When a guy drew an extra rank bull and needed all the encouragement he could get, what did his girl do? More likely than not she would start spilling tears and begging him to pass, afraid he might get hurt. If a guy tried to work three rodeos in one week, spending his sleeping time driving back and forth, his girl would sometimes do her best to talk him out of it, not understanding that a guy had to work more than one rodeo at a time to make enough money to qualify for the world championships.

It was not that Byron had anything against women in general--he fully intended to marry and settle down someday. It was just that as far as he was concerned, women and bull riding just didn't mix, and until his bull riding days were over, he had no time for females.

As he sat on the fence watching his bulls eat, he was disgusted with himself for the way he had let this Wilder girl get under his skin. Anybody who could ride half a dozen bulls every day ought to have the discipline to keep a hazel-eyed, black-haired girl like Karen Wilder out of his mind--and that's just what he intended to do.

Byron heard the rumble of a truck in the driveway. He hopped off the fence and hurried to the door leading to the unloading chute. Karen was driving the truck.

To Byron's surprise, she was already backing up to the chute. Most women would have moved away from the steering wheel and let a man do the backing, but she was perfectly content to do it herself, and to Byron's surprise she knew what she was doing. She got it right the first try.

Karen swung down from the high cab, offered a

quick hello in stride, then climbed quickly to the top
of the chute to open the tailgate. Byron was impressed
with her quickness and competence in performing her
task.

She was wearing the same faded blue jeans she had
worn the day before and a brown down ski parka. Her
boots were covered with black rubber overshoes,
unsnapped at the top, and she wore a white western
hat, not a fancy new one like the barrel racers wore,
but a more practical-looking one she had probably
worn for years in working on her father's ranch.

Realizing he was staring, Byron forced himself to
look away from the woman to the big grey-brown
cows that were thundering down the chute. Byron
went inside to head them to the bucking chute and to
get things ready for the afternoon rides.

After moving the truck out of the driveway, Karen
joined Byron. She had a clipboard under her arm, and
to Byron's surprise, she was being accompanied by a
chubby fellow with thick glasses and a receding
hairline. Byron hadn't noticed the fellow earlier, who
apparently had been seated on the passenger side in
the cab of the truck while the cows were being
unloaded.

"Byron," said Karen, "I'd like you to meet a friend
of mine, Claude Benson."

"Pleased to meet you," lied Byron, shaking the
chubby hand.

"Claude has a dental practice in Springville," said
Karen.

"Love you cowboys," grinned the dentist.
"Cowboys make me a lot of money--the ones that get
kicked in the mouth by bulls, steers and wild horses."

Byron felt an immediate dislike for the dentist. The
fellow wasn't bad-looking, except for the chubby, soft
look from lack of physical activity. Byron wouldn't admit to himself that perhaps he felt a wave of jealousy
at seeing another man with Karen.

"Dad and I made up an evaluation sheet for recording the cows' bucking performances," said Karen, nodding towards the clipboard. "If you don't mind, Claude and I will stick around and fill out the report while you ride." She looked into Byron's eyes as she spoke.

"Stay if you like," said Byron with mixed feelings. While he liked the idea of Karen watching him ride, the presence of the dentist annoyed him. "But I can keep the records if you two have other things to do."

"No, we'll stay," said Karen. "Dad wants me to keep the records, at least for the first little while...."

"And I want to stay too," interrupted the dentist. "Maybe I'll pick up a little extra business if one of those cows kicks you in the mouth." He laughed loudly at his own joke. Byron and Karen didn't laugh.

"Suit yourself," said Byron as he climbed to the top of the bucking chute, where the first cow was waiting to be ridden. The rigging was already in place.

Quickly, Byron lowered himself onto the cow's back, took a firm grip on the rigging, then reached for his improvised rip cord to open the gate. When he jerked on the cord, nothing happened. The system was jammed somewhere.

"Gate won't open. Someone's probably been fooling with the ropes," said Byron as he loosened his grip on the rigging.

"Hang on," said Karen. "I'll get the gate." She started to climb the fence after handing the clipboard to Claude, who remained in a safe place behind the fence.

Byron's first impulse was to tell her not to do it. He didn't want someone on the gate who didn't know what they were doing. Someone might get hurt. But the girl moved confidently and quickly like she knew exactly what she was doing, like she had done it many times before.

When Byron gave the signal, Karen swung the big

gate open at just the right speed and the big cow lunged into the arena. Byron hung on with one hand, the other waving over his head, for about fifteen seconds before letting go and hopping to the ground. The cow had bucked moderately well, but nothing to brag about.

Byron hazed the cow out of the arena. By the time he arrived back at the chute, Karen had the second cow ready to go. She asked Claude to hand her the clipboard.

"What was the number on that cow's ear tag?" she asked.

"Sixteen," said Byron.

"I'll give her five points. We'll rank the others in relation to her, a higher number if they buck harder, a lower number if they don't buck as hard," she explained as Byron secured his rigging to the second cow.

Karen was all business, keeping score, moving animals into the chute and opening the gate. With her help, Byron was able to proceed quickly from animal to animal. At the end of two hours he had ridden eight cows and three bulls. Claude remained safely behind the fence, occasionally repeating his joke about the money he would make if Byron got kicked in the mouth.

Several of the cows scored very well. One a fifteen and one a seventeen. The rest were below ten. One received a zero. When the gate opened, this cow merely trotted into the arena as if there were no rider on her back. She ignored Byron completely. Even when he applied the spurs, she refused to buck.

The cows that scored above five remained in the arena for more riding. Those that scored below five were loaded back into Karen's truck.

Chapter 14

Karen came to the barn three or four afternoons a week to help Byron with his riding and to evaluate the cows. Except for that first visit when she was accompanied by Claude Benson, the dentist, she was alone-- and that was fine with Byron. He liked having Karen around, though there was little idle time with keeping the records, loading the chute, and opening the gate. The riding, with the accompanying details, seemed to go smoother when Karen was around.

On the average the cows didn't buck as well as bulls, but there were a few exceptional ones that bucked better than many of the bulls used in the big rodeos. These were the ones that were earmarked to become breeding stock in Morton Wilder's experiment to develop a superior breed of bucking bulls.

One evening as Byron was browsing through his riding records to see if there were any particular bucking patterns that tended to be more difficult for him to handle, he noticed something very surprising. Charted over a period of many weeks, less than a fourth of his spills occurred on the days when Karen was present at the barn, and she had been there most days. The more he studied the figures, the clearer it became that he rode significantly better when Karen was there than when she was not.

Byron scratched his head in disbelief, but he couldn't argue with the charts. He wished he could have a talk with the little man in the mountains, the Wasatch Savage. He would probably have something insightful, at least interesting, to say about the reports. Too bad The Savage was so hard to get to, especially in the early spring when the trails leading to the tops of the mountains were still under deep snow. Byron decided to present his findings to Karen, and had to admit to himself that he felt more than a little excitement about doing it.

The next day was one of those brilliant spring afternoons when, after a series of 45-degree cloudy days, the sun finally appears and the temperature soars into the mid-sixties by early afternoon. It was probably the warmest day since the previous October, the kind of afternoon when everyone wants to be outdoors.

Karen quickly agreed when to her surprise the always serious and all business Byron suggested they take a break from the bucking practice and go out into the afternoon sunshine.

Sweet-smelling new green grass was beginning to push through the quickly warming soil. The ground was nearly covered with little buttercup-like flowers, blooming close to the ground. It appeared that the very pebbles were turning to blossoms under the magic sunshine of the first spring day as Byron and Karen worked their way up the rocky hillside behind the barn.

When a rocky ledge blocked their path, Byron jumped up first, then offered his hand to Karen. She didn't really need his help, but she took his hand anyway and held on a little longer than necessary.

They worked their way to the top of the little hill and found a resting place among some large boulders. They sat down with their backs against a huge sun-warmed boulder. Byron picked up a piece of sage and began scratching designs in the soft soil. There was a long silence in which neither of them spoke. Their shoulders were touching.

Byron was the first to speak.

"Last night while I was going over the bucking

records I made an interesting discovery," he said. Both of them were looking at the stick as he continued to carve designs in the dirt.

"What was it?" she asked quietly, without looking up.

"My chances of getting bucked off were about four times as great when you weren't around."

"You're kidding," she said, surprise in her voice. She looked up at Byron.

"No. I'm dead serious," he responded, still looking at the stick. "Do you have an explanation?"

"Probably has something to do with me opening the gate for you," she responded quickly. "Allowing you to better concentrate on your grip and what the bull or cow might do."

"That might account for some of the difference," said Byron, "but not a four-to-one advantage."

"Then what do you think is the reason?" Karen asked, somewhat taken back that he had discounted so quickly her suggested explanation.

Byron hesitated a moment, still playing with the stick, then throwing all caution to the wind he said, "You being there, watching me, that's the difference. I do better when you're there."

"Oh, I see," said Karen, laughing. "Like I'm a rabbit's foot, your lucky charm."

Byron broke the stick in two and slung the pieces out into air. They clattered on the rocks below. He turned to look at Karen. "I don't believe in lucky charms, and I don't think you do either," he said with conviction.

Karen was looking down now, at the marks Byron had made in the dirt. "I understand what you're saying," she said in a quiet, serious tone. "And you should know I feel the same way about you. Otherwise I wouldn't have spent so many afternoons helping you ride." She looked up into his face. Nothing was said for a long time. Karen was the first to look away.

Byron tried to take her hand. She pulled it away.

"I'm not interested in becoming a bull rider's girl," she said, "tagging along from rodeo to rodeo. Not again."

"You don't understand..." said Byron, but she cut him off.

"No. You don't understand," she began. "My mother died when I was 14. It was in Great Falls, in a hospital. Our stock was at a rodeo there. We were always on the road in the summer, going to the different rodeos, Dad, mother and I.

"There were lots of young, good-looking bull and bronc riders around and Mother was always cautioning me to stay away from them. I'm sure she told me that at least once a day that summer before she died.

"After she was gone I gradually forgot, or tried to forget, her advice. By the time I was sixteen, some of those young, dashing bull riders began to be interested in me.

"There was one in particular. I met him at the big rodeo in Calgary, the Stampede."

"Hey," interrupted Byron. "You don't have to tell me about your old boyfriends."

"I'm going to tell you about this one, whether you like it or not," she insisted, emotion in her voice.

"His name was Dusty Williams. He was 20. I was almost 17. It was love at first sight, for both of us. He followed Dad's stock around that summer, winning more than his share of the prize money. He was just a kid, doing it for the fun and excitement. He wasn't fanatical about it, like you are.

"When he won, he spent all the prize money on me, buying me presents, taking me to the best restaurants. When he got hurt he came to our trailer, where I doctored his wounds and bandaged him up.

"That summer was the happiest time of my life. I was in love with Dusty and that's all that counted. I probably wasn't much help to Dad."

"Why are you telling me all this?" asked Byron.

"Because it all ended very suddenly," she said, "the second night of a three-day rodeo in Fargo. Dusty drew a bull called Black Thunder. The animal went into a mean spin and Dusty couldn't hang on. I'd seen him take a lot worse spills, but there was something wrong in the way he hit the ground. He didn't get up."

Karen paused for a moment. The emotion was gone from her voice and face.

"When they loaded him into the ambulance he was screaming about not being able to move his arms and legs. His neck was broken. He died the next day."

"I'm sorry," offered Byron.

"All that night I kept hearing my mother's words of warning, again and again," she continued. "After Dusty's death, I resolved to never get involved with a bull rider again. Never." She looked into Byron's eyes. "I've kept that resolution, and I don't intend to break it now, not for you or anyone else."

"Nobody's asking you to," said Byron, standing up.

He looked down at her. "Thanks for coming down to the barn to help me with my riding. It's meant a lot to me. Maybe when the season's over, I'll call you."

"That would be great," she said, "but nothing serious, not as long as you're riding bulls."

"Nothing serious. I promise. But if I make the world championships in Oklahoma City, I'll be quitting at the end of the season."

"I won't believe that until I see it," responded Karen. "You might end up a few dollars short in your winnings. Then you'll want to try again next year. Or you'll break an arm or a leg. That'll end things for you this season, but there's always next year for every bull rider I've ever met."

"Look," said Byron, suddenly becoming angry. "I

wasn't proposing marriage. You've been a big help to me and I was just thinking that you and I made a pretty good team. I was wrong. I didn't know how you felt about bull riders."

Byron wasn't through.

"I intend to become a world champion bull rider. I'm the best. I don't know of any rider who has ever been better prepared than me going into a new season. Nobody has worked as hard as I have. I've averaged five or six rides a day for five months. I'm in perfect condition. I feel more at home on the back of a bucking animal than I do talking to you." He paused, gathering his thoughts for a final statement. "It appears to have come to a choice between you and bull riding. My choice is bull riding. I will not be turned away."

Byron started back down the hill. Karen followed behind. When they came to the rock ledge, he didn't offer her a helping hand as he had on the way up.

When they arrived at the barn Byron helped Karen load the remainder of the her father's cows into her truck. No words were exchanged as they worked. When the cows were loaded and Karen was climbing into the cab, Byron said, "Thanks for helping with the riding and record-keeping. I'm sorry things didn't work out better between us."

"So am I," said Karen as she started the engine and shifted into low gear. Byron stepped back as the truck lurched forward.

Chapter 15

After Karen stopped coming to the barn, Byron
reduced his riding program to two or three bulls a day,
just enough to keep up his muscle tone. He obtained
maps of the United States and Canada and began plot-
ting the locations and dates of the biggest rodeos.
Beside the location of each one he wrote the amount
of prize money that would be awarded the winners.
Qualifying for the world championships was based on
earnings, so the name of the game was to ride in as
many of the top-paying rodeos as possible. Sometimes
that meant entering two or three different rodeos on
the same weekend, driving back and forth between
events--many hours on the highway and very little
sleep. Some of the top bull riders even had single-
engine airplanes which enabled them to cover more
rodeos on any given weekend. Byron spent plenty of
time working on his Dodge Power Wagon, replacing
parts, tuning it up. He couldn't afford time-consuming
repairs once the rodeos began.

Several weeks later as Byron was putting the
finishing touches on his schedule, he received an
unexpected telephone call from Karen. He could tell
by the tone of her voice when she said hello that
something was wrong. There was a pause. He waited
for her to speak.

She told him that her father had died of a heart attack the previous afternoon while unloading a ship-
ment of hay. The nearest blood relative was her
father's brother in Alaska, who wouldn't be in town
for several more days. Karen said she needed Byron's

help with the livestock, the feeding and other chores, while she handled the arrangements for the funeral. Byron said he would be glad to help.

The next three days Byron spent most of his time at the Wilder ranch tending the livestock. Claude Benson, who drove a silver Chevrolet Blazer with white sidewalls, was there too, but the dentist spent little time around the barn and corrals and did nothing that could be described as work. He did manage to repeat his joke to Byron several times, the one about how much he liked bull riders because of all the business they brought his way when bulls kicked out their teeth.

The funeral was short and simple, the way Karen thought her father would have wanted it. The people who attended were mostly rodeo people who had worked with Morton over the years. The funeral was conducted by the local Mormon bishop, an old friend of Morton's. Karen's father hadn't been much of a churchgoer, especially in the summer when he was on the rodeo circuit. Still, the bishop had some very kind things to say about him.

They buried Morton Wilder in the Evergreen Cemetery on the bench southeast of Springville. It was a beautiful day, a few scattered clouds moving slowly in a warm spring breeze across a deep blue Utah sky. The warmth of spring had already turned the grass green, and flowers were beginning to bloom.

After the grave was dedicated the people began to leave two and three at a time. Karen asked Claude to hurry back to the ranch to make sure everything was ready for the buffet luncheon scheduled for family members and close friends after the funeral. She stayed at the grave until the last of the guests left. Only she and Byron remained.

"What am I going to do?" she asked as they turned from the grave and began walking to Byron's truck. Maple Mountain had never looked more beautiful, still white with snow at the higher elevations, but lush and green below the snow line.

"What do you mean?" asked Byron as he caught up to Karen and walked beside her.

"I'm now the owner of the nation's top string of bucking bulls scheduled to start appearing at rodeos in about four weeks. How can I do it without Dad?"

"Hire someone to do it for you," said Byron matter-of-factly.

"That's not as easy as it sounds," responded Karen. "Dad's tried that before, and it always got us into trouble. There are so many things that go wrong-- stalled trucks, injured bulls, poor facilities like no water and broken-down fences at rodeo locations. You can't just hire any old cowboy to handle those kinds of problems consistently. The first thing you know, your stock doesn't make it to a rodeo on time, word gets around, and you have a tough time getting bookings for a couple of years.

"The only way to run a successful bucking string is to be with the animals yourself all the time. You've even got to sleep with your stock and I guess what frightens me as much as anything are all those creepy guys that hang around rodeo grounds at night, those drunks. It's scary."

They stopped walking and turned to face each other.

"Claude says I should sell the bulls," she said.

"Maybe you should," said Byron, trying to be helpful, but not sure he was saying the right thing. "What do you want to do?"

"I don't know," she said, emotion in her voice.

Without thinking, Byron reached out, taking her by the shoulders and drawing her to him. She didn't resist, welcoming his strong arms around her, pressing her tear-stained cheek against his shoulder. It seemed a long time to both of them before any words were spoken.

"Maybe Claude is right," suggested Byron. "Maybe you ought to give some serious thought to selling the bulls."

"Then what would I do?" she said, pushing away from him. "Live happily ever after as Claude's wife? That's what he's proposed."

Byron was taken back. He had figured Claude was serious about Karen, but he hadn't guessed things had gone so far.

"What do you want?" asked Byron. "Do you want to marry the dentist?"

"Maybe. How would you feel about it if I did?"

"How I feel doesn't really matter," he responded quickly. "Since your plans and mine don't mesh anyway. If you think Claude will make you happy, I suppose you ought to marry him."

Byron could tell by the twisted expression on Karen's face that she didn't like his answer. He waited for her to speak.

"Dad worked too long and too hard building that bucking string," she began, turning away, "for me to just up and dump the whole thing five minutes after he's gone. No, I've got to keep it going. At least I've got to know I tried. Can you understand that?"

"I think so," responded Byron.

"It's one thing to fail and have to bail out," she said. "At least I tried. But to sell out without even trying--I don't want to live with that."

"Then don't," said Byron. "Go for it. You know the business. I think you'll succeed."

"What about Claude?"

"Let him marry one of his nurses," said Byron. "You don't love him anyway, or do you?"

"I guess not," she smiled, turning to look at Byron.

"Good," said Byron. "Then you won't be mad at me for what I did to him yesterday."

"What?" asked Karen, grinning at the sudden change in the direction of their conversation, welcoming the shift to a less serious subject. "What did you do?"

"I shouldn't have done it," said Byron, looking down at his boots, beginning to regret he had said anything at all.

"Tell me," insisted Karen.

"I was checking out some of the headgates at the upper end of the big pasture," he began, still looking down at his boots as he kicked at a burdock weed. "There was some water in the main ditch, so I turned it into the pasture to see how it would flow. When I went back to shut it off, there were these two big old carp that had come out into the pasture with the water. They were dead, probably poisoned by someone upstream trying to get rid of weeds."

"Why are you telling me this?" asked Karen impatiently. "What do those carp have to do with Claude?"

"Don't know. Just reminded me of him. Maybe their mouths."

"That's a mean thing to say," chided Karen.

"I put them in a gunnysack and stuffed it in the spare tire compartment of his silver Blazer."

"You didn't!" exclaimed Karen, holding one hand over her mouth, beginning to laugh.

"Shouldn't have done it," said Byron, grinning too. "Not with the funeral coming up. But seeing that Blazer, just parked there all afternoon, knowing Claude was in the house with you when you probably wanted to be by yourself, just made me a little mad, or jealous, I suppose. I shouldn't have done it."

"Did he find the fish?" asked Karen.

"Not before he left," said Byron, "and the windows were closed and the sun was shining on the Blazer all afternoon. But I did notice that when he drove off last night, his windows were rolled down."

"That's why he came in a different car to drive me to the funeral this morning," she said. "But he didn't say anything about the fish."

"Maybe he hadn't found them yet."

Karen suppressed the urge to laugh some more.

"Come with me," she said, catching Byron by surprise. "We make a great team, working with livestock. We could become partners. There's a great future in bucking bulls, especially if the selective breeding with the cows pays off. Let's do it together."

"Stop," said Byron, backing up a step. "We've been down this road before. Remember that day on the hill." His voice was firm.

"I've worked too long and too hard at my bull riding to give it up," he began. "Why don't you sell your bucking bulls and come with me? We make a great team. You do the driving, I'll do the riding. We'll split the take. We'll have a great summer together. My first rodeo's in Las Vegas. We could even make it all legal by going to one of those marriage places."

Karen began laughing again, giving Byron hope that perhaps she was softening in her resolve against teaming up with a bull rider.

"Why are you laughing?" he asked.

"I suppose because we are so much alike," she said. "Can't you see the great future we could have together? Everything I have--the bulls, the ranch, the bookings--can be yours too."

"I'm a bull rider and don't intend to give it up until I've won a world title in Oklahoma City," insisted Byron. "I'm after a little revenge too. If not during the regular season, I expect I'll get another chance to ride Medicine Bull and dig my spurs into his ugly hide. I'll ride him this time."

"No," she said, shaking her head vigorously. "I can't have that be a part of my life. Remember what I told you about Mother, about Dusty?

"Can't you see, Byron?" she pleaded, hands on hips, feet apart. "It's such a fleeting, hollow dream. It'll all be over for you in a year or two. Sure, you'll probably make good money while you're at it, and get

your picture in the papers because you won a big
purse or got hurt real bad. But when it's all over, what
will you have? A few grimy trophies and a broken
body that will ache and pain you the rest of your life.
Next time you get on a bull I hope it throws you and
breaks both your arms. Maybe that will put a little
sense in your thick skull."

"Something is wrong here," said Byron, staying
calm but shaking his head. "On the one hand you talk
like you can't live without me, but on the other you
belittle my lifelong dream and ambition to become a
world champion bull rider. The pain, the sacrifice, the
work, the injuries. I've paid the price. I'm ready now
to culminate the dreams and work of a lifetime. And
you want me to give it up. I can't and won't do it."

"My life is at a major turning point with my father
in the ground over there and the rodeo season beginning in a few weeks," Karen said softly, fighting to control the emotion welling up within her. "I need you
now, not next year when you've got this bull riding
thing knocked out of you."

"I need you too," said Byron, not giving any
ground to her pleading. "With you along I'll do a lot
better. As you said, we make a great team. Come with
me this year. Next year I'll retire and we'll take the
stock around, and the year after. But now I must
ride."

"The bookings are for this year," said Karen, her
voice beginning to sound tired.

With their differences still unresolved, Byron and
Karen walked back to his pickup. He drove her to the
ranch but did not stay for the buffet. Neither slept
very much that night.

Byron called her early the next morning.

"Have you changed your mind about coming with
me?" he asked as she picked up the receiver.

"No," she said simply. "I was hoping that maybe
you had changed yours."

"I haven't," he said. "But Karen, after thinking about yesterday, it seems somehow there must be a way to resolve our differences. We seem so right for each other."

"What do you suggest?"

"I don't know," said Byron. "I'm going into the hills for a few days. To see an old friend. Maybe I told you about him. I call him The Wasatch Savage. I'll call you when I get back. Maybe with the passing of a little time we can figure something out."

"I wouldn't count on it," said Karen, "unless you want to give up your bull riding."

"No dates with the dentist while I'm gone," added Byron. "Well, at least not in the silver Blazer, unless you like three-day-old steamed carp."

"No promises," Karen laughed, "but you don't need to worry about Claude."

"I won't," said Byron. "See you in about a week." He hung up the phone and headed towards the barn to find his snowshoes. There was still plenty of snow in the high country behind Spanish Fork Peak.

Chapter 16

On a partly cloudy evening in April, 1983, Byron pushed his way over the crusty snow that covered the trail on the back side of Spanish Fork Peak. He had been on the trail most of the day and was enjoying a vigorous workout in the crisp spring air. His destination was the rugged canyon where Chester Peabody's cave was located. He hoped The Savage was still there, that he hadn't moved to a new location.

Byron wanted to have a talk with The Savage. There was something simple and straightforward about the little man, an ability to look to the core of things, to slash away the unimportant trivia and see clearly the heart of matters. He was probably a little bit crazy, living alone in the wilderness like he did, but somehow Byron couldn't help but feel there was a stroke of genius in the seeming madness.

Byron was making good time over the crusty snow. Being late in the season, the snow was hard and crusty, seldom breaking beneath the snowshoes. The sun was still shining when he reached the top of the rugged canyon.

Ahead of Byron six elk blocked the trail, including a five-point bull that hadn't lost its horns yet. The elk had been grazing on a south-facing slope where the sun had melted off all of the snow. When they saw Byron coming, they didn't spook like they would have during the fall hunting season. After a long winter of deep snow, scarce grazing and no hunting pressure, they had lost much of their wildness. As Byron moved closer, those that were lying down stood up, and as

Byron got even closer, the elk gradually moved up the ridge to let him pass but didn't scamper out of sight.

Byron didn't stop to watch the elk. He pushed ahead, hoping to reach The Savage's cave before dark. He noticed the big rock where he had discovered The Savage shouting at the distant mountains.

The cave was further down the trail than Byron remembered, but he wasn't worried about getting caught on the mountain after dark. With a new moon, mostly cloudless sky, and as much snow as there was, he knew he wouldn't have any trouble following the trail, even after dark.

It was almost dark when Byron left the trail and headed up into the section of rocks and timber where he remembered the cave entrance to be. Soon he discovered what appeared to be a well-beaten path leading from the cave to the water below. Then he smelled fresh pine smoke.

Assured The Savage was still living in the cave, Byron quickened his pace. As soon as he could see the mouth of the cave, Byron cupped his hands around his mouth and shouted, "Chester, are you home?"

The surprised Savage greeted him at the mouth of the cave. "If it isn't bull rider Byron Horn," he said. "Didn't expect to see you again, at least not before the snow melted."

The Savage took Byron's hand in both of his and shook it warmly. Byron followed the little red-haired man into the depths of the cave.

The cave was warmed by a blazing fire in the stone fireplace. Everything was the same as Byron had remembered it--the table with the books, the shelves of food, the deerskin cot. The only difference was the greatly diminished supply of firewood.

Byron slipped out of his pack and leaned his snowshoes against the cave wall.

"Hungry?" asked The Savage.

"What's in the pot?" asked Byron, looking towards

the black kettle on the flat cooking plate built into the rock fireplace. He wanted to know what was cooking before he admitted how hungry he was.

"Sweet and sour beaver dumplings," said The Savage enthusiastically.

"Can't say I've ever had that before," ventured Byron cautiously.

"My own recipe," boasted The Savage. "It's so good I've been eating it every day for three weeks. I'll toss in a couple of fresh dumplings."

The Savage reached for a wooden bowl about half full of sticky white dough. He removed the lid from the steaming kettle and dropped four big globs of dough into the bubbling stew, then returned the lid.

Quickly he cleared some papers and books off the little table and set out two tin plates, spoons, mugs, salt and pepper and a pitcher of water, which he filled from a water bucket.

Byron pulled up a chair, a two-foot section of a big log. It wasn't long until The Savage brought over the steaming kettle, scooped out a big dumpling for each plate, then poured the sweet and sour beaver over the top.

Byron's first bite was small. The stew smelled good, but he was still not sure he would like the strange new food. He found it tasted as good as it smelled. His appetite, dormant from a hard day on the trail, was aroused quickly, and it didn't take him long to polish off three helpings of The Savage's concoction.

"That's good stuff," said Byron, now that his appetite was satisfied. "How do you make it?"

"Nothin' to it," said The Savage. He was obviously pleased that Byron liked his cooking. "Just throw a hunk of meat or a carcass in the pot and boil it all afternoon until the meat is falling apart. You can use about any kind of meat. The old Indian favorites were buffalo tongue, moose nose, bear paws or beaver tail.

But if you can't get these, there's a lot of other things that work good too--deer, porcupine, grouse, muskrat and squirrel. When you use the smaller rodents, it takes longer to fish out the bones once the meat's cooked, but it still tastes pretty good when finished.

"After the meat's cooked and all the bones are out, I dump in a few handfuls of dried chokecherries--they make it sour, about the same amount of dried thimbleberries or gooseberries--that's where most of the sweetness comes from, though I usually add some store-bought sugar. I always throw in a fistful of wild onions, season with salt and pepper, and simmer for a few more hours. You can serve it over potatoes, noodles, rice, bread, or just eat it plain, out of a soup bowl."

"Sounds easy," said Byron. "I'll try it at home sometime with beaver or elk--but you can keep your muskrats and squirrels."

"A muskrat eats the same things a beaver eats and tastes about the same too, only the pieces are smaller," said The Savage, trying to defend the more exotic variations of his recipe.

"When's the last time you ate a candy bar?" asked Byron.

"About a year ago," said The Savage. "I hiked down to Thistle and had a Milky Way."

Byron reached into his backpack. "Brought you a whole bag of little Snickers," he said. After opening the bag and taking one out for himself, Byron tossed the rest over to The Savage, who immediately tore the wrapper off one of the little bars and tossed the whole thing into his mouth.

"Almost forgot what a candy bar tastes like," mumbled The Savage, his jaws working furiously. He didn't say another word until he had finished off his fourth bar.

"If I'd known you were so crazy about candy bars, I'd have brought more," said Byron, glad he'd been able to please The Savage.

"There's a lot of things a guy misses when he lives alone in the wilderness for a few years," said The Savage thoughtfully. "If you'd brought a gallon of tossed green salad and a quart of ranch dressing I could have eaten it all at one sitting. Or a dozen peanut butter and jelly sandwiches, or a 20-piece bucket of Kentucky Fried Chicken, or a couple of Big Macs or Whoppers, or a half gallon of ice cream.

"I miss my wife too," continued The Savage. "Even the nagging and bickering sometimes seem better than being alone. And I'd chop ten cords of wood to be able to watch the Super Bowl or the NBA basketball playoffs on color television. Once you get used to things, it's tough to get them out of your system. You know how tough it is for people to give up cigarettes. Living up here, I've had to give up hundreds of things other people take for granted."

"Why don't you go back?" asked Byron.

"Don't misunderstand me," said The Savage. "I'm not complaining or admitting I made a mistake. I'm glad I live this way, at least for the present. I'm just describing how it is sometimes, how I miss things I used to have. But I wouldn't go back. Not yet. I haven't finished what I came here to do."

"Yes, I noticed that mountain is still there, the one you were trying to move," said Byron. "Have you given up on that?"

"No. That was Billies Mountain. Solid rock, I found out. I decided to start on something a little easier, a softer hillside across the main canyon."

The Savage looked away, beyond the entrance of the cave. It was like he'd forgotten he was talking to Byron, and was thinking out loud.

"I've learned some things here," he said quietly. "You don't just tell a mountain to get up and go and have it happen, no matter how great your faith. It's more than that. Like everything is part of a very fine

or spiritual force--people, animals, trees and bushes--
even the rocks and mountains have a finer spiritual
being.

"When all the spiritual forces from all these things
flow together in harmony, powerful things can happen. But when they are in disarray, without any
unified flow, there is nothing. The key is to sense or
feel the flow, the forces, and be in harmony with
them. When you learn to flow and bend with the
forces around you, they in turn begin to flow and bend
with you. That's the source of real power."

Byron wasn't sure he understood what The Savage
was trying to say. Nevertheless, he didn't ask any
questions. The Savage seemed to be on a roll, the
thoughts and feelings flowing freely, and Byron didn't
want to interrupt.

"It starts with little things," said The Savage, continuing to look past the entrance of the cave into the
black night. "Like helping a calf elk out of a rocky
crevice so it can return to its mother, and later being
able to touch that elk as it grows to maturity. Like
moving a rock so a young plant can have more sunshine, then watching it grow larger and healthier than
those around it that have had plenty of sunshine all
along. Like walking around a rattlesnake instead of
killing it, because you have a silent pact with it and its
species not to harm each other. Killing only to live, not
for sport, and showing reverence for the kill by valu-
ing and using every part of it and not letting anything
go to waste. By not disturbing that which does not
need to be disturbed. By listening for that which the
ears cannot hear--not for seconds and minutes, but for
hours and even days, until the silent secret flow of the
force can avoid you no longer. Then gradually becoming part of it, first by hearing, giving and bending with
it. Moving with the flow, becoming one with it. Then,
and only then, can you begin to influence and direct
the flow. And only a little at first. It is hungry for

human intelligence, but afraid, wary of human abuse. And you can understand why.

"And those first times you direct the force, the majesty overwhelms you. Like the first time you caress a wild animal or command a fierce wind to soften its bite and it obeys. You drop to your knees, overwhelmed by it all. You are physically weak and unable to stand. And to know you are barely on the threshold is almost more than you can bear."

Byron wished he had a tape recorder. Whether The Savage was a raving lunatic or an inspired genius, it didn't matter. Byron only knew that The Savage's words left him with a hungry feeling. Not a hunger for food--a hunger to see beyond locked doors somewhere deep within, doors he hadn't noticed before, not until the words of The Savage, like keys, began rattling in the locks.

"And you are on a threshold too," said The Savage, turning, smiling warily, like he had said too much and wanted to change the subject to something more comfortable. "You are about to become a world champion bull rider."

"Is that prophecy or flattery?" responded Byron, feeling relief for a break from The Savage's intense monologue.

"Neither," said The Savage. "Only a statement...if that's what you still want to do. Is it?"

Byron paused. "I think so," he said finally. "But there are some complications."

He told The Savage about his riding program, how he had ridden half a dozen bulls a day, and how when fresh bulls became hard to come by he had taken in Morton Wilder's big cows to test their bucking ability, so Morton would know which cows to use in developing a superior breed of bucking bulls. He told how he had come to know Karen Wilder, Morton's daughter, through the cow riding program. He explained the discovery he had made in studying the bucking statistics, that he was able to ride better when she was watching.

"Do you think that might have something to do with the flow, both of us in harmony to the point where she could help me stay on those bulls, even though she was standing by the gate?" asked Byron spontaneously.

The Savage nodded, but said nothing.

Byron told The Savage how he had fallen in love with Karen, and she with him, and about her insistence on not getting involved with another bull rider. He mentioned the death of Morton Wilder, leaving Karen alone with the ranch and one of the most sought-after bucking strings in the country, scheduled to be on the road in just a few weeks. She needed a man to help her. Byron.

"I love her," said Byron, "and I really want what we can have together. But I feel too much water will pass under the bridge this summer if we go separate ways, me riding bulls, her taking the stock. I have this uneasy feeling that with me and Karen, it's now or never."

"What do you want to do?" asked The Savage.

"As I said, she won't have me unless I give up bull riding. She knows how much it means to me, how hard I've trained to become a world class rider, but she won't budge an inch. She had a boyfriend once who was killed riding bulls, and I guess she's afraid that'll happen again."

"Maybe it will," said The Savage.

"To me?" asked Byron.

"Maybe she's more in tune with the force than you think. Some women tend to be that way, you know."

"I don't want to give up my dreams," said Byron. "All that work, the hardest training program ever undertaken by a bull rider. I've got to see if I can do it. I can't just quit, not after everything I've done."

Byron paused for a minute or two, looking into the

fire. The Savage remained silent.

"I can't do both," said Byron, looking at The Savage. "Had her father not died, we could have both gone our own ways and gotten together again at the end of the season. It would have been easier for me to quit then, after I had made my run for the world title."

"But her father did die, and things are different now," said The Savage. "She needs you now. A year ago I would have told you to forget the girl and go for the championship. Now I'm not sure that's the best advice."

"Do you think I should give up bull riding, so I can be with Karen?" asked Byron.

"I can't tell you to do that, not tonight. Maybe in the morning." The Savage yawned. "I'll bet it's long past midnight."

After throwing a few more sticks on the fire, The Savage retired to his cot and Byron to the deerskin bed.

Chapter 17

The next morning after a breakfast of warmed-over sweet and sour beaver stew, Byron and The Savage went outside and hiked to a sunny rock. They were both in meditative moods and not many words had been exchanged.

The rock quickly warmed to the morning sun. There were no clouds in the sky, and it was one of those beautiful spring days when a lot of the snow on the rugged mountainside would melt.

"Why do you want to become a world champion bull rider?" asked The Savage.

"Don't know if I can put it in words," replied Byron thoughtfully. "It's just something I've always wanted, ever since I was a kid. I was good at bull-riding, so I thought a lot about it."

"Who else in this world cares about you becoming a world champion bull rider?" asked The Savage.

Byron had to think about this question a moment. His parents didn't want him to ride bulls--too dangerous, and no future in it. Karen didn't want any more to do with him if he was going to be a bull rider. What anyone else thought really didn't matter much.

"Nobody, I guess, except maybe you, and I'm not sure how important bull riding is to you, after last night," said Byron.

"I don't care about bull riding as a sport," said The Savage. "I would attend a rodeo to see you ride because I know you, but my interest doesn't go beyond that. Why do you do it, Byron?"

Before Byron could answer, The Savage asked, "Is

it money?"

"No."

"Is it fame, having people whisper behind your back, 'There goes Byron Horn, the famous bull rider?'"

"No."

"Why do you do it, then?"

Byron kicked away a piece of loose rock as he thought about The Savage's question.

"I guess there's a feeling of satisfaction and accomplishment in being able to do something that most other people can't do. The idea of setting a goal to be the best in the world at something, and reaching that goal, is pretty exciting, at least to me. Is that bad?"

"Not at all," answered The Savage. "But I think the struggle, the striving against odds, is where the value is. The excelling, the striving to do something better than it has ever been done before. After all that training, do you think you're the best now?"

Byron nodded. "I think I am, and I want to prove it."

"To whom?"

Byron had to think a second. "To me."

"Who else?"

"Not Karen, my parents, or you. Just me, I suppose."

"Does the best rider always win the most money and the world title?"

"Not necessarily. Sometimes there's sickness, injury, family obligations and any number of other reasons why a guy is held back from making it to the top. Sometimes just bad luck--drawing easy bulls that make it impossible to score enough points to win."

"If you were hurt in a car wreck and couldn't ride this year, would you still think you were the best?"

"There would always be doubts, not being able to prove it."

"To yourself?"

"Yes."

"Is there a way to satisfy yourself that you are the world's best bull rider without going on the riding circuit this summer?" asked The Savage.

"I don't know of any way," said Byron.

"How would you like to know you are the best, and have Karen too?"

"That would be nice, but I don't know how I can have both, without her bending some."

"I do."

Byron looked at The Savage. "What are you getting at?"

"The answer is very simple," said The Savage, choosing his words carefully. "All you have to do is go home and ride Medicine Bull. You said all the top bull riders in the world had chances to ride him last season, and all of them failed. He is the best bucking bull in the world. If you can ride him, you will be the best rider, certainly if no one else rides him this year. If you can ride Medicine Bull, you won't need to spend an entire season following the rodeos. Medicine Bull is your shortcut to the top. Ride him and you'll know you're the best. Then you can give up bull riding and marry Karen. Everything you want will be yours."

Byron was laughing. "You make it sound so simple. Just ride old Medicine Bull, the bull that's never been ridden, the bull that not only injures half the cowboys who try to ride him, including me, but has killed a few too. 'Just ride Medicine Bull' you say, like it's as easy as falling off a log. You don't know what you're talking about. You certainly don't know anything about bull riding."

"Are you afraid of Medicine Bull?"

"No, but I have plenty of respect for him."

The Savage stood up. He was angry, his face red. He pointed his forefinger at Byron.

"Look," he said, almost threateningly. "You're the

one who said you were the best bull rider in the world. If you are, prove it by riding Medicine Bull. I don't know if you can. I don't know if you are as good as you say you are. I've never seen you ride. But if you can ride Medicine Bull, you won't care what I or anyone else thinks, you'll know you're the best whereas now you are just guessing."

There was silence again. Byron stood up. He had always thought there would be a chance of his drawing Medicine Bull later in the season at one of the big rodeos or at the world championships. It could happen. But to try to ride that bull now, without a draw, that made him uneasy.

Byron knew, too, that there was a lot of truth in what The Savage said. Medicine Bull had never been ridden. The bull would try to kill him as it did every rider, but if he succeeded in riding the white bull, even outside an official rodeo, Byron would know he was the best. Trying to ride Medicine Bull would be the ultimate test, where all Byron's work and training would receive the final irrefutable evaluation. Perhaps he would fail. Perhaps he would die. Perhaps he would succeed.

"Thanks for the advice, and the stew," said Byron, the tension gone, the smile back in his voice. "If I ride that bull I expect you to move that mountain."

"A deal," said The Savage. Byron turned and headed back to the cave to get his snowshoes.

Chapter 18

The afternoon sun was warm on Byron's back as he reached the lower elevations of Spanish Fork Peak and stopped to remove his snowshoes. He had already taken his coat off and tied it around his waist. The perspiration on his forehead felt cool in the fresh spring breeze. It was hard work pushing through the slushy snow, even downhill. But the exertion felt good as an escape from the burden that now weighed heavy on is mind.

He selected a huge flat boulder and sat down to remove the snowshoes. Finished, he gazed back at the rugged canyon leading to the top of Spanish Fork Peak. The warm sun, the cool breeze and the majestic mountains filled him with a sudden sense of well-being that was enhanced by the knowledge that he might not ever be able to enjoy it again--not if he attempted to ride Medicine Bull, the animal that had injured more riders in one season than any animal in the history of bull riding.

Byron remembered the first time he had tried to ride Medicine Bull and how badly he had been injured, the long recovery, the hard work and training to get back in condition. He thought about Karen, a new dimension to his life, her stubborn unwillingness to get involved with bull riders.

Byron contemplated The Savage's suggestion that he ride the great bull now. Even the thought of it made his palms sweat and caused a sickening feeling in the pit of his stomach. He figured Karen probably wouldn't cooperate with him in an attempt to ride her famous bull, so he would have to do it behind her back. If he succeeded, would he be able to give up bull riding and team up with Karen? On the other hand, if he failed he would prove nothing, but Byron found it hard to concentrate on the consequences of losing. Swallowing hard, Byron secured the snowshoes to his pack and continued his journey down the trail.

Two days later, it was well past midnight when Byron and his brother Billy turned up the dirt road leading to Karen's ranch. All the lights in the house were out. The only source of light was the night light on the power pole near the front of the barn.

About a quarter of a mile from the ranch, Byron turned off his headlights, turned off onto the shoulder of the road, and parked his pickup. After removing the bell from his braided bull riding rigging, Byron and Billy crawled through the barbed wire fence and headed across the open field towards the pole corrals behind the barn. Billy carried a stopwatch and a flashlight.

It was a clear, cold night, a quarter moon just over Spanish Fork Peak to the east. Thousands of tiny stars crowded the black sky.

The wet sod was spongy as their feet crunched through the already frosty grass. The warm days had brought all of the winter frost out of the ground, but the muddy surface still froze some nights like the crust on a pie. This was one of those nights.

Byron made special note of the ground condition, knowing the corral would be the same but muddier because of the lack of grass. If and when he was thrown, it was reassuring to know the mud was soft beneath the frozen surface crust. Falling on solidly frozen mud was worse than falling on concrete. Frozen mud wasn't any harder than cement--it was just its rough, irregular surface that made it worse.

The two walked silently, side by side, through the

field. It was Billy who finally verbalized what both were thinking. "What do you want me to do if he throws you and comes after you?" he said.

After a short pause Byron responded, "Hop into the corral and try to draw him away, but stay close to the fence. He's as quick as lightning. Whatever you do, don't yell at him. Don't want to wake up anybody."

Byron forced his thoughts away from the potential injuries that might be awaiting him. This was no time for negative thinking. He contemplated his training and conditioning program. Every muscle in his body was tuned perfectly for bull riding. After a long winter of training he was better prepared to ride this bull than anyone had ever been before. He was the best bull rider in the world, about to ride the best bull in the world. But was he really the best? He would know for sure if he rode the great white bull for the required eight seconds.

"Remember there's no ambulance," whispered Billy, "so be extra careful."

The adrenalin began to ooze quietly into Byron's bloodstream. His heart quickened, his eyes dilated. He unbuttoned his jacket to relieve the increasing warmth flowing through his body.

They found Medicine Bull in his usual corral just outside the rear entrance to the barn. When they looked through the rail fence at him, he returned the stare with mild interest, not with any degree of alarm. It was almost as if he had been calmly waiting for them. His tail twitched carelessly from side to side although there were no insects in the frosty night air. It was like he was a big cat eyeing his prey.

Byron and Billy had no trouble coaxing the great white bull through the series of corrals leading to the bucking chute. He had been there before, all 2,000 pounds of him, and didn't seem to mind going again. His glossy white coat was stretched tight over his steel-hard muscles and glistened with beauty and grace as he moved forward through the sparse moonlight. The bull's gauntness of the previous fall was gone. A winter of rest and feed had allowed him to build more muscle and reserves. He was stronger and heavier now than he had ever been before. He was ready for the upcoming season.

When the two cowboys came to him in the night and began driving him towards the bucking chute, he gladly complied with their demands. He had been growing restless in the close confinement of his private corral and welcomed the chance to buck with a cowboy on his back for a moment or two. It would feel good to stretch his legs again in an open arena. His massive body quickly warmed to the excitement of battle and the thrill of the chase. Actually, the great Medicine Bull usually spent more time chasing cowboys than he did trying to buck them off.

When the last gate was closed quietly into place and the bull was secure in the bucking chute, Billy gave Byron a worried look. "Sure you want to go through with this?" he said.

Byron nodded.

"Sure we got the right bull?" asked Billy. "This one is awful quiet, not kicking and fighting like I thought Medicine Bull would."

"That's him, all right," assured Byron. "He's quiet because he's too smart to waste his energy fighting the chute. When the gate opens he'll explode."

Byron was standing directly above the bull now. He lowered one end of his braided rigging down the far side of the bull. Billy reached under the animal's belly with a straightened coat hanger, hooked the end of the dangling rope and drew it underneath. Byron cinched the rigging to just the right tightness, being careful not to get it too tight because the bull's chest would expand when the animal began bucking.

Next they secured a rope around the bull's flanks

and cinched it tight. Byron didn't think the flank strap
was necessary on Medicine Bull. The bull would buck
his hardest with or without the flank strap. Byron just
wanted his ride to simulate actual rodeo conditions as
closely as possible.

When everything was ready, Byron looked at Billy,
who said, "You don't have to do it, you know."

"Don't open the gate too fast. I want his nose headed straight out into the corral," said Byron, ignoring
Billy's comment.

Byron lowered himself to the bull's back. Billy
climbed reluctantly into the corral to open the gate.
The stopwatch was in his hand. The night light in
front of the barn offered just enough light to allow him
to see the hands on the clock.

As Byron wrapped the braided end of the rigging
around his left fist, he felt the pounding of his heart as
it pumped a fresh burst of adrenalin through his body.
There was a warm, strong feeling throughout his
body. All his muscles had a pleasant ache as if they
were itching for action, and they were.

Byron could feel the warm strength of the bull
through his thighs. He wondered if the bull was feeling the same anticipation of excitement and possibly
danger.

Byron was ready now and a thousand thoughts raced through his mind. He could remember clearly his
first attempted ride of Medicine Bull, how easily the
bull had thrown him, then smashed him beneath its
pounding hooves. Byron's months of intensive training flashed before him, as well as his love for Karen,
the cause of this crazy attempt to ride her bull.

Byron dug his spurs firmly into the bull's
shoulders. The spurs were not the jingling kind used
by bronc riders, but blunt-end spurs that hung onto an
animal rather than rolling off the shoulders.

The bull didn't flinch at the pressure of the spurs.
To him the feel of the spurs didn't mean pain, only a

signal that the gate was about to swing open. He was ready and waiting.

"Let him out, Billy," said Byron.

Time stood still. First there was the clank of the bolt as Billy jerked it free. Then the squeaking of the hinges as the gate swung out. As the gap opened from two feet to four to six, the bull remained frozen. He knew from dozens of similar experiences the previous season just when to make his move.

The gate was nearly half open when with the quickness and grace of a wildcat, Medicine Bull spun and lunged into the small arena. Byron leaned back, dug in with his spurs and hung on with all his strength.

The animal that had been so quiet in the chute was now a demon of wild fury--twisting, turning, lunging, spinning. Never the same move twice, never any consistency that a rider could depend on. There was a rage and madness in the bucking, as if the bull had been storing up energy for this encounter all winter.

Byron rode like he had never ridden in his life. Several times during those first few seconds he started to lose his seat, but each time he managed to regain his position.

Realizing he had no ordinary rider on his back, the great white bull increased the furiousness of his bucking, hurling himself recklessly across the corral, gaining momentum and speed as he did so.

With each passing second, Byron's spirits soared higher and he hung on more desperately. Several times it felt as if his arm would be jerked from his body, but he refused to release his grip and somehow managed to keep his seat. His months of intensive training were paying off. On this quick, aggressive bull, there was no time for thinking and pondering. Everything Byron did was by reflex, automatic reactions developed over hundreds of practice rides.

It could have been a result of the bull's mad fury,

the darkness of the night, the corral being smaller than a regular rodeo arena--or a combination of all these factors. At the end of the sixth second the bull crashed into the pole fence at the far side of the corral.

The two middle rails, unable to withstand the two thousands pounds of flying bull, snapped like rifle shots. The top rail struck Byron across the side of his head and he felt a sickening crushing sensation in his right knee. Both bull and rider lost balance. There was a long moment of helplessness as gravity pulled them down, followed by the sudden jolt of the spongy semi-frozen mud and the scramble for footing. Byron took advantage of the momentum of his fall and, instead of trying to get up, merely converted the energy of his fall into a roll towards the fence, where he scooted to safety under the bottom rail just as the bull regained his footing. Medicine Bull trotted to the center of the corral, snorting hot steamy breath in the crisp semi-darkness.

Byron lay on his back, breathing deeply, trying to read the sensations of pain that his body was sending to his brain. He moved his fingers to a sharp pain in his chest that intensified at the touch of his fingers. A cracked or broken rib, nothing to worry about. He had had broken ribs before and knew it would be a lot more painful in a few days, but that it would eventually heal by itself with little or no medical attention.

Next he checked out his knee, which made him nauseous with pain. He raised his leg, allowing the knee to bend. He kicked his foot up and down a few times. The knee seemed to be working all right; it was just a little smashed and bruised on the outside. He raised his hand to the throbbing side of his head and pulled it away again when he felt the warm stickiness. His palm was black with blood. He reached back and carefully probed his scalp with his fingers. The wound was only on the surface, again nothing to worry about.

Byron sat up. He could hear voices and see

flashlights coming towards him from the house.

"You all right?" whispered Billy.

"A few cuts and bruises but nothing serious," responded Byron. "How many seconds before we hit the fence?"

"Six, exactly." said Billy. "Thought you were going to make it all the way. Better get out of here before they catch us."

"This way," whispered Byron, motioning for Billy to follow him. Moving as quickly and quietly as possible, they crawled under another fence and buried themselves in a pile of straw.

Soon Karen and her uncle, who was still in town, were at the corral examining the broken fence and Medicine Bull. The bull was still wearing the flank strap, so it didn't take them long to figure out that someone had attempted to ride the animal.

From his bed of straw, Byron could hear Karen's voice. "Probably the result of a dare between a couple of drunken cowboys," she said. "From the looks of that fence, I'll bet they won't try it again."

After looking around for signs of the midnight bull rider, and finding none, Karen and her uncle removed the bull's flank strap, tossed it over a fence, tied up the broken rails, then returned to their beds.

A few minutes after all the lights were out, Byron and Billy climbed out of the straw and brushed themselves off.

"Let's get out of here," said Billy. He started for the field, but when he noticed Byron wasn't following, he turned back.

"What's wrong?"

Byron was shaking the straw off his braided rigging while staring between the rails at the great white bull. After a moment he spoke quietly, yet firmly. "I came here to ride that bull and that's what I intend to do."

Billy could hardly believe his ears. "You mean you're going to ride him again?"

"Yeah, help me get him in the chute."

Reluctantly Billy agreed, and within ten minutes the white bull was again in the bucking chute. This time, however, Medicine Bull wasn't as peaceful as he had been the first time. He bumped restlessly about in the narrow enclosure and several times kicked back sharply at the plywood door behind him, causing a loud bang to shatter the quiet of the night air. Byron and Billy looked cautiously each time towards the house, expecting the lights to go on. But the house remained dark and Byron continued to get ready for the second attempted ride of the evening.

The braided rigging was in place when Byron cinched up the flank strap. Annoyed at the pain, the bull struck out with both hind feet at the plywood door. This time the lights in the house were turned on.

"Let's get out of here," said Billy.

"Hurry. Get down by the gate," ordered Byron. "I've got some unfinished business with this bull." Billy obeyed.

"Got the watch ready?" asked Byron as he lowered himself onto the bull's back.

"Yeah," grunted Billy. "Hope that guy doesn't have a shotgun this time."

Byron quickly wrapped the end of the rigging around his left hand and wrist, then looked away towards the house. Karen was running towards the corral, shouting behind her for her uncle to join her.

When she reached the fence, Byron shouted, "Karen, don't come in the corral, we're about to turn the bull out."

She stopped, momentarily unable to recognize Byron's voice. Then she suddenly realized what was happening.

"Byron Horn," she shouted, "What in..."

Her voice was cut off by Byron's loud command. "Open the gate, Billy."

The gate swung open and the angry bull lunged into the   corral--twisting, turning, spinning. In a wild rage the beast fought savagely to throw the determined Byron, who hung on with a strength beyond his natural limits. It was only through sheer willpower that he was able to hang on when there was enough force to pull his arm from its socket.

Byron felt his grip weakening. The braided rope slipped an inch or two through his fingers. He fought desperately to tighten his grip, only to feel another inch slip away. He was filled with a sickening feeling, knowing he would soon be on the ground and there was nothing he could do to prevent it. The rope slipped again.

As if it were a mile away, he heard a shout, Billy's shout. Byron knew there was only one thing that would make Billy yell like that. The clock had passed the magic eight-second mark.

Joyfully, Byron let go of the rope and was instantly launched into a looping orbit. He caught a glimpse of the bull turning to meet him when he hit the ground, but there was nothing he could do to alter his course.

Byron landed on his hands and knees. At the same instant the bull butted him solidly in the ribs and knocked him into a sideways roll, the momentum carrying Byron under the fence before the bull had time to hit him again. It was over.

Byron lay on his back, eyes closed, savoring the knowledge that he had ridden the great white bull, the animal that had never been ridden before, for eight seconds. His lifelong ambition to be a world champion bull rider, as far as he was concerned, was at last accomplished. Now he could turn to other things.

"Byron?"

He heard Karen's voice just a few steps away but, thinking she might still be angry about his riding her bull, kept his eyes closed and didn't move. Better to let her worry away her anger before she found out he didn't have any serious injuries.

She sat down beside him and cradled his head on her lap, rubbing away the smeared blood with the corner of her coat and shouting to her uncle to call an ambulance.

"I don't think there's anything broken," muttered Byron. "Don't call an ambulance. I'll be okay."

"Byron, I thought you were still in the mountains," she said. "The mountain started moving and blocked the road. I figured your way was blocked and you wouldn't be out for a while."

"What?" questioned Byron.

"You haven't seen it on the news--right across from Billies Mountain, a whole mountain slipping down, blocking the road and damming up the river."

"No kidding!" shouted Byron. "So The Savage did his thing too."

"What are you talking about?" demanded Karen.

Byron didn't hear her question.

"Say, I've been thinking," he began. "We could train a mean-looking old bull to ride like a horse, to play dead and do a bunch of other tricks. The clowns could ride him out of the chute. The act would really be a crowd pleaser. What do you think?"

"What are you talking about?" said Karen. "Are you sure you're all right?"

"Never felt better," responded Byron. "You just witnessed my last competitive bull ride. I've ridden Medicine Bull. I'm the best in the world. I don't need to do it anymore."

"Do you really mean that?" asked Karen, hardly unable to believe her ears.

"Yep," said Byron cheerfully as he struggled to his feet. "Help me get cleaned up. Got to find that bishop as soon as it's daylight."

As the tears welled up in Karen's beautiful dark eyes, she threw her arms around Byron. He pushed her away.

"What's wrong?" she asked in surprise.

128   The Wasatch Savage

"Hugging hurts like crazy. Got a busted rib."

A smile spread across her tear-stained cheeks. She leaned forward and carefully kissed him on the cheek. Arm in arm they started towards the house.

"Do you think I could have done it if you weren't there watching me?" asked Byron.

"Never," answered Karen with confidence.

"You know," began Byron. "We could also take one of those cows I was riding, one that really knows how to buck, and add her to our string. The libbers would really go for a bucking cow, and could you imagine the embarrassment of the cowboys she throws...."